MILLION DOLLAR DEATH

A Novel

By

Alexandra Y. Caluen

Credit where credit is due ...

This novel owes a lot to the developmental input of my sisters, R.K. and K.K. To the extent that grammar crimes and syntactical villainy persist, they are entirely my doing.

Alexandra Y. Caluen

Million Dollar Death

I: Tanith

It's part of the lingo, you know. "That show nearly killed me." We don't mean it literally, we just want to draw attention to how hard we work and (incidentally) start a conversation about our work. Because there's nothing we like more than to talk about our work. For one thing, how will anyone hire us if no one hears about our work?

But getting back to my point.

This is a story about what happened when a show was, literally, murder.

It was finally happening for me, after years of working on other people's shows, gradually moving from high school to college to black box to actual, real theaters. Years of walk-ons and staged readings and bit parts and chorus and here-and-thereian, a few second leads and ingénues and then a couple of leads. Then an assistant-director gig, reading every play I could get my hands on, and studying filmed plays like my life depended on it, which it kind of did.

That's an exaggeration, of course, because nobody needs theater to survive. Some of us need it to retain our sanity. And a few of us need it to create a world that we can at least pretend to control. I was doing a good job pretending I was in control, for a minute there.

I'd stolen time here and there from my day job, and written a full-length, musical play of my own. I'd packaged it for myself to direct. I'd lined up a cast and crew. I had funding (thanks to Kickstarter). And I had a theater. I was going to Broadway.

Not *that* Broadway. Let's be serious.

1

I live and work in L.A., and the 'theater district' here is spread over a 200-square-mile area; maybe more. There are nice theaters from Pasadena to Redondo Beach and everywhere in between. But for me, this was a big deal; it was a big play – not 'Starlight Express' big, but local big - and it needed a big theater. A big theater, that is, that wouldn't cost me a year's rent. So with a lot of wheedling and some finagling and maybe a little cleavage, I had two consecutive weekends – Friday through Sunday, four shows each weekend including a Sunday matinee – at the Million Dollar Theater on Broadway in downtown L.A.

I had a crew lined up to handle the box office, minibar, and souvenirs. A friend designed our program and another friend was producing a cast recording. We had well-photographed lobby cards (not just copies of my actors' head shots), and our dress rehearsal was going to be recorded so we could post the dance numbers on YouTube. I'd been calling in favors – and debts - for a year.

My cast list had been set for a month and a half and nobody had dropped out. All of the key roles and professional dancers were being paid; all the crew - even the prop master and the wardrobe mistress – were also being paid. (This was triply good for me because the prop master and the wardrobe mistress were my housemates.)

I also had a supporting cast of volunteers, recruited from the local dance community. The play, you see, was set in a dance hall. I called it a play in song and dance, because it wasn't a traditional musical but the songs (and dances) were essential. So I needed people who could dance, and by dance I mean social dancing. I couldn't have afforded all professional ballroom dancers even if they would have committed to the show, so I was using amateurs.

The strong ballroom community in L.A. wasn't unknown to me. I'd been happily surprised all the same to get as many proficient dancers as I had. The thing with using volunteers is, they can't look like amateurs onstage or they'll pull the eye from the main action. You don't want your audience looking at a background player and wondering why they are there. You want them looking at the leads and following the dialogue.

Anyway, it wasn't a huge cast. It was like this:

Leading man; leading lady; villain; ingénue; featured dancers; showgirls; bar staff, waiters, and a cop; and social dancers. It was a story about a cop who's undercover as a bartender in this bar-slash-dance hall, because all of a sudden it's eating young girls. And about a woman who's looking for a particular young girl who may have been seen there.

We'd done six weeks of readings and scene rehearsals, and we were in the final week of prep. I had somehow contrived to get all twenty-eight scenes (plus prologue) and all fourteen songs (plus instrumentals) locked down, and the songs recorded. Frankly, I have no idea how anyone managed to produce a show before the Internet, smart phones, and GPS.

We'd worked in a dance studio and a classroom and a rehearsal space out at the Brewery, and had finally started working in the theater. For a lot of my people, it was the first time they'd worked anywhere that had not only raked seats out front and a curtain on the stage, but dressing rooms backstage. The social dancers had been so cute the night before. It was the first time on any kind of stage for all but one of them, but they had been thoroughly attentive and involved.

3

My only problem with them was getting them to mime their conversations on stage.

I told them, "Decide approximately what you're going to say to each other--the same basic stuff every time--and when you're not here, you can practice it together talking out loud. But on stage, we need to be able to hear the singers and the speaking parts, so you can't make a sound."

They all nodded their comprehension, and immediately forgot. I enlisted my prompter, a woman who'd auditioned for social dancer but couldn't really hack it, to also be a shusher. She was doing great, and because they all felt sorry for her not getting to dance, they were obedient.

Where was I? Oh yeah.

My lead guy, Tony, was knocking my socks off on a daily basis. His counterpart, Jenny, was doing great. My ingénue had gotten a standing ovation from the cast and crew for her big number the previous night. But my villain, oh, my villain. He was the silky, sexy superman of seductive evil. He was so good I was pinching myself.

I was also kind of kicking myself, because I hadn't given Victor (the actor playing the villain) nearly enough to do. But it's one of those things: the play can only be so long, and the focus needs to be on the story. The unexpected gift of show-stopping talent must sometimes be (regrettably) underemployed. How was I to know a guy who played a cop on a TV show notorious for overexplaining things (I mean a typical scene was Cop: exposition, Cop: exposition, Commander: concerned look, gruff order recapping exposition) could ground a performance with practically no words?

Okay, I'll admit it, I cast him for looks, and for his singing voice. I did the same thing with my leads. The fact that all of them could truly act was a bonus.

They'd all been great throughout the weeks of rehearsal. The supporting cast had been – or at least, had become – solid. Everyone had learned their lines, everyone had been punctual. But now it was opening night minus four, and one of my key people (who happened to be my villain's understudy) was missing.

I called Kevin, my stage manager, on the walkie. "Have you heard from Billy? He's on the call sheet today."

"Nada."

"Did you call him?"

"Twice."

"Shit." I thought for a minute, then decided we needed to play it through. "Well, Red's up." Red, my prop master, was the fill-in for the two parts played by Billy, and I'd rehearsed him just in case. That's one of many things that is simpler when your swing player lives in the same house with you.

Kevin said, "On it," and I knew it would get handled. We did the scenes and Red was fine. I was worried about Billy, though – it wasn't like him to miss a rehearsal, especially this close to opening night. Anytime you expect somebody reliable and they don't show, you go to the worst case scenario, or at least I do. Plus, we were already pretty thin: the cast wasn't exactly swarming with extra bodies, or to be more accurate, all my extra bodies at this point were non-professionals.

You see why we say a show is killing us?

Earlier that day, I'd had lunch with a friend who had helped us out with rehearsal space (she also happened to be the mother of my ingénue). I remembered, now, that she had mentioned seeing Billy with Victor during rehearsal breaks a couple of times. She'd said they were talking pretty intensely. I hadn't really thought anything of it – what else did these guys have to do during a rehearsal at a high school? – but I thought I'd have to ask Victor about it later. Maybe Billy hadn't been happy with the show, and hadn't wanted to tell me. I had to put that away, though.

This was our first tech rehearsal. So we were running set changes, and song and dance numbers, which meant most of the show. Our sound guy and our music person and our lighting person were fine-tuning their cues. The tech wizard doing our lighting was also working projected backdrops. We had only a few built set pieces, set pieces being something that productions with actual money get. But we needed to set the scenes, and a friend of a friend knew a guy who did computer art and they came up with what I thought were really cool backdrops. We still had some kinks to work out, like where to put the projector. The backdrop projection had to hit the scrim and not the actors' faces, without getting washed out by the lights.

Anyway.

There we were, running a number, when a bunch of clompy feet came down the aisle and someone said, fairly loudly, "I need to talk to whoever's in charge here."

I thumbed my walkie and told Kevin to cut, then turned around, ever so slightly furious. "We pay by the hour here, you know."

"Are you Tanith Salazar?" It was a good-looking Latino guy in a sport coat and slacks. Right behind him were a tall bony black guy and a shorter Latina, similarly dressed.

I was getting a bad feeling. "Who wants to know?"

"L.A.P.D."

I heard a "whoa" from the stage and thought, now would be a good time to be nice. "Yes, I'm Tanith Salazar. How can I help you?"

"I'm Detective Ysidro Palacio. It's my understanding Mr. Billy West was working for you."

"Yeah, Billy is ... wait a minute, did you say *was* working for me? That's wrong. He *is* working for me. He's one of my actors." The bad feeling was getting worse. The no-show plus the 'was' combined to give me a sensation close to nausea. I would have known, I thought; someone would have told me. If something happened, wouldn't I have heard? Why hadn't I heard? This had to be some kind of mistake. I felt a hand on my shoulder.

Valerie, my music producer. "Tanith," she said softly.

The cop's voice was a touch softer too, when he said, "I'm sorry, Miz Salazar, but Mr. West was found dead this morning at his home."

I: Ysidro

I'm not sure what I was expecting. It had been a long day and my team was tired. We still didn't have our tox screen back and we'd had to come all the way from Van Nuys to downtown because that was where Billy West's grief-stricken husband had sent us. He said, all the people Billy was working with are going to be down at the Million Dollar Theater. He said, please find out what happened. He said, Billy just had a physical and he never took drugs.

To which we said, We'll let you know what we find out. Because when a cop finds an otherwise-fit middle-aged guy face-down on a couch with an empty coffee cup on the floor beside his limp hand, well, that cop tends to think of drugs.

The house had been a model of domestic order. The only thing out of place was the dead guy. And the sweep had turned up nothing more suspicious than a bottle of organic compost tea under the kitchen sink. But there are more different ways to die from drugs than most people think.

Kyong Song had come out to the living room bright and early, having gone to bed early, as he always did, he said. West wasn't due home until around midnight, because of the play he was working on. Song never waited up, he said. He was a sound sleeper. He'd been surprised to wake up alone. And then he went out, and found what he found, and called 911.

Washington and Muñoz, the others on my team, both tried to be subtle about calling and texting their

8

spouses after we left the house. I don't know why they bothered hiding it. I wished I had someone to call.

It was dinner time when we got to the theater, but we'd done the drive-thru at Jack in the Box, so at least we weren't starving. We'd been at it since eight, though, and like I say, I don't know what I was expecting. But I sure wasn't expecting Tanith.

When she turned around I felt like someone hit me in the gut. She looked like she was designed by somebody at Disney. She was little, curvy, big-eyed, pretty, and young. And black. I must have thought a theater director would be older, or bigger, or whiter, or something.

She looked at me like I had told her somebody ran over her dog. "Not Billy," she said. Her big Bambi eyes filled with tears.

"Were you close?"

"He was a family friend." There were four people in that group, in the middle of the orchestra section. Why they called it that, I don't know. A Japanese guy, and an older white guy, a white woman, and Tanith. The white woman had her hand on Tanith's shoulder.

I'd learn who they all were soon enough. "And Mr. West was working with you on this show?"

"He was one of my key people. He was part of the process from the very start. Oh, God."

A tall red-headed guy came down from the stage. "What's going on, Tanith?"

"Red, the detective says Billy is dead." Tears were streaming down her face.

The tall guy dug out a bandanna and handed it to her. "What happened?"

"You are?" I said.

"Drew Warner. Call me Red."

"Thanks. We're not sure yet," I said. "We're waiting for a toxicology report. But it looks like an overdose."

"That's impossible," said Tanith, from inside the bandanna. "Billy didn't even take aspirin."

"We'll know more tomorrow. In the meantime, we're treating it as a suspicious death, and we need to interview everyone who saw Mr. West yesterday. How many of your cast and crew are here tonight?"

"Most," said Warner. "Twenty. Well, nineteen."

"I can get you the complete list and contact information," said Tanith.

"We had everyone here yesterday for our first full run-through," Warner added.

"And tonight you're doing what?" I addressed the question to the tall guy. It was easy enough to see why he went by 'Red': his ponytail was two feet long and approximately the color of V8.

"First tech."

Whatever that meant. I made a note to look it up, if I had to. "Where can we set up to do interviews?"

Tanith pulled herself together. "Is it all right if we keep running with whoever you're not talking to?"

One of my team leaned over and suggested quietly that if the show was going on, people wouldn't be sitting around speculating. I thought that was a good point.

"Sure." I thought for a second. "Detectives Washington and Muñoz will be doing a physical investigation of the theater. They'll try to stay out of your way." Sam and Teresa, my team, nodded stoically.

10

"You could use the makeup room," said Tanith. "It's backstage right and it has a door."

"You want to go first, Tanith?" asked Warner. "Then you can carry on."

"Yeah, okay. Tell Kevin we need to call a break, don't tell anybody what's going on." I almost said something about how we needed to make sure everybody came back, but I realized she needed them even more than I did. If anybody bailed, she'd make sure I knew who, and she'd know where I could find them.

Warner was saying, "They're going to be all over me."

"We've only got the space till midnight. We have to focus." She pressed her hands to her eyes for a moment, and took a visibly deep breath.

"Yeah, I know." Warner loped back up to the stage and I saw him talk to a slim black guy who'd been standing at the front of the stage, watching us. The black guy called a fifteen-minute break. Tanith and the others in her group got out of their seats and came out to the aisle. The white woman patted her again, and said something in a low voice. Tanith shook her head. There was a general exodus for the front of the theater. I guess the El Pollo Loco across the street was about to get a rush.

Washington and Muñoz headed for the stage, determined to get a good look at that before everybody came back. I waited for Tanith to blow her nose and get herself together. Then we went up to the stage. She turned left.

"I thought you said backstage right?"

"I did. It's right if you're on stage looking out."

I turned around and looked out at the seating, as if I were an actor. I got it. From my new vantage point, both sides had arrangements for curtains or whatever to be pulled across. Sets of pulley systems were anchored to the floor, each masked from the audience by a narrow panel of curtain.

Looking up, I saw a complex rack of lights and other fixtures, bordered by a square of slender catwalk. I didn't see how anyone would get up there, but figured Muñoz or Washington would sort it out. Probably Muñoz. Sam didn't like heights.

Up in the right corner was a cage of electrical controls. As we approached that, a small seating area opened up on the right. It was well back of the pulley things, separated from them by a narrow unmarked passage leading to the emergency exit door.

I was walking behind Tanith and thought everyone was gone, so I was startled when she spoke to somebody. "Hey you." Her voice sounded warm.

"Who's there?"

"It's the cat. He's not supposed to be in here. I saw him yesterday, hanging around in the alley."

"The back door's unlocked, right?"

"Yeah, and of course it's not alarmed. Somebody probably went out for a smoke, and let him in."

She pointed to the door. It was unimpeded and appropriately marked, and sure enough there was a cat sitting in front of it. He got up and walked over to Tanith, rubbing against her leg. She bent down to pet him and I got a clear view of his backside, leaving no doubt about gender. He had patches of black and orange with a white chest, and grey tabby stripes over everything. He was a mess, but he was big and friendly and I heard him purr. I started to like the cat. "You going to put him out?"

"No. I'm going to give him a snack."

I was amused. "So he's not supposed to be in here, but you're feeding him?"

"A theater cat is good luck." The cat followed us into the makeup room, which smelled indescribable. Tanith put a paper dish on the floor and filled it with kibble. Then she filled the top of a thermos with water and set it down. The cat thumped her leg again and settled in to eat. We took seats next to the makeup counter. She wrapped her arms around herself, a gesture I'd seen many times on occasions like these. Literally trying to hold herself together.

"I apologize for this," I said. "I understand you're upset. We'll get through it as fast as we can." She nodded once. I looked around the room. "What's with the smell?" I was trying to identify it. "Did you do makeup tonight?"

"No, all the hairspray and greasepaint over all the years has kind of soaked into the space. This theater is almost a hundred years old."

"No kidding."

"Okay, so what do you need to know?"

I took her through the basics of her identification, her relationship to West, his part in the production, and the events of the preceding day.

"So we wrapped up at eleven-thirty. My crew and my leads stayed another fifteen minutes for notes and then we all went home. Billy was understudying a second lead, so he stayed."

"Did Mr. West have a coffee cup with him?"

"Yeah, he always did."

"Did he have a particular drink he liked?"

"Chai tea latte. So sweet, ugh."

I made a note. "And how long has he been with Mr. Song?"

"They got married last year, but they've been together for thirty years. They went to New York to see a few shows, Billy had so many friends there, and got married. They were so happy." Her face crumpled a little.

"Do you happen to know how they met?"

She sniffed. "They were both working for Warner Brothers. Kyong was a gardener and Billy was a contract artist. That's where Billy met my mom, too – she works in casting."

This jibed with what Song had told us earlier. "I may need to speak with your mother."

"Oh man, really? This is going to be tough on her." Tanith didn't argue, though. She gave me her mother's cell number and address.

"And what is it you do when you're not directing a play?"

"You mean my day job? I'm a voice artist for a couple of the production groups at ABC/Disney."

"Like for animation?"

"Yeah. Amazingly, there's not a huge on-screen market for short curvy women who happen to be black. Unless you want to constantly be victim of the week."

"I'm guessing victim isn't your favorite role."

"I'm so sick of all these crime shows, I can't even tell you."

"I feel the same way," I told her, with perfect honesty.

"But then here I am directing a crime story where women are victims," she said, with irony. "What do you like to watch?"

"The Amazing Race. Survivor. Like that. How about you?"

"I like to read."

I nodded and moved on. "Could I get your residence address for the record?"

She recited it for me, then added, "I live there with Red and Lesley. That's Lesley Hayes. They're prop master and wardrobe mistress for the show. And Red's my swing player. That means if someone doesn't show up he can step into several parts."

"And what's your relationship?"

"We're all just friends," she said. "We're all single right now. Red and I discussed having a fling early on, but decided we were better off keeping it, you know, Platonic."

"You discussed it, huh?" I said, hiding a smile, but didn't pursue it. I was pretty sure that was the first not-true thing she'd said. If it turned out to be important we could straighten it out later. Now was not the time. Hardly anybody tells the whole truth to the cops.

II. Tanith

I'm in the business of talking, so that part of the interview wasn't hard. And the detective – he told me to call him Sid – was certainly easy on the eyes. He looked like a cross between young Andy Garcia and Paolo Montalban. I was glad I'd worn the orchid-colored, beautifully-fitted safari vest Lesley had made for me (and picked out for me that day, saying "you need pockets"), instead of the gray tank top I'd almost paired with my jeans.

The hard part was finishing a piece of the conversation and suddenly remembering why we were having it. I was glad we were in the makeup room, because there were packets of tissues everywhere.

He was a good interviewer. I'm sure he got more out of me than I intended. He asked me about voice work, and I did some of my voices and sound effects for him. It cracked him up. He asked me how I got into acting. "Well, it was my mom. Working at the studio, she kind of had an in."

"Yeah, I see that."

"She started me off with commercials, background, and print work."

"And background, that's what exactly?"

"Extras, non-speaking parts. People in the background."

"Gotcha."

"Then I did the High School Musical movies and stuff like that, where they needed a big cast. And at least those ABC/Disney casts are not whitey white white. But at a certain point they couldn't really keep casting me as a teenager, and there's not much else out there."

16

And then there was a knock on the door. Sid went to open it. It was Red. "Everybody's back, Tanith." He was looking at me with concern. I did an 'I'm okay' thing behind Sid's back and saw that Red registered it.

"We're done here for now," said Sid. "Miz Salazar, you can do your thing. If you would just send back the next person."

I thought, for now?, and threw him Red. Then I went out to start running the group numbers.

We ended up going a little later than I'd hoped, thanks to people being in interview when their scene came up, but still managed to finish the rehearsal before midnight. I made sure the cat was back outside, locked the fire door, and turned to see Sid behind me.

"Miz Salazar, I'd like to speak with you and your housemates in more detail tomorrow if that's possible."

"Anytime between ten and four," I said, knowing all I really had to do tomorrow was damage control, and an update on the project page. Oh yes, and contact my Henchman and tell him he was now understudying three parts. "As far as I know, Red and Lesley are in all day too."

"Thanks. I'll give you a call after ten. And I'm sorry for your loss."

We shook hands and then Sid collected his two partners. Red joined me at the front of the stage and we watched them go. Then we dismissed everybody, reminding them that second tech was on Wednesday starting at seven.

"Please don't talk to anybody about Billy," I said. "At least until we have a better idea what happened. I'll contact the rest of the cast early tomorrow."

Everybody said they agreed, but I had a feeling a bunch of texts had already been sent. After the others were gone, Red and I did a walk-through to make sure there wasn't something stupid being forgotten like a plugged-in curling iron that would burn down the theater. The dressing room looked especially creepy. "I was so happy to get this place," I said mournfully. "Now it's skeeving me out."

"Chin up," Red said, putting his arm around my shoulders and giving me a squeeze. "It's still your baby. I like this place, personally. As crusty as it is, it's got style."

"You did good tonight," I said, changing the subject. "We've got to figure out your costume, though. You and Billy are not even close to the same size. Oh fuck it all." He still had his arm around me. I turned and pressed my face against his chest, trying not to cry. He wrapped his other arm around me and, because he knew me really well, didn't say anything sweet. After a few minutes, I had myself in hand and eased back.

Because he was awesome, he went straight to what we'd been talking about. "Lesley and I'll take care of it tomorrow. Cross your fingers Marco doesn't have to step in."

"Oh shit, I know." We made our way back up to the stage.

"So, did the detective ask you if we were, you know?"

"He didn't exactly ask, but yeah. I told him we discussed it and decided against." Which of course hadn't been the truth.

"Discussed it, huh. That's one way to describe it."

"I didn't think I needed to give him details. What did you say?" I gave him a sidelong look.

He gave me a fondly exasperated look in return. "I told him that I was nursing a hopeless passion for you."

Thank you, I thought. "Well sure, isn't everybody?"

He snorted. "If I told him that you drive me crazy on a daily basis, would that clarify?"

"Not necessarily." We double-checked the tech box and headed out to the lobby.

"I wonder if he asked Lesley." He followed me out the front.

"God, I hope not." Lesley hadn't been in college with us, but we'd all been friends a long time. What she didn't know about us, nobody knew.

That was pretty much a terrible night. It hadn't been so bad at the theater, where I was busy. At home, alone in my room, all I could think about was Billy.

I ended up taking Zzz-Quil so I could sleep, and woke up all groggy when my alarm went off at eight. After a couple of cups of coffee and about fifty emails to and from cast members – sure enough, everybody including the social dancers knew about Billy – I was more or less clicking. I had just gotten off the phone with Marco Hidalgo – my Henchman - when the detective called, at five minutes past ten.

"We have the tox results," he said after a brief greeting. "Mr. West died from an overdose of oxycontin."

"What? I don't believe it."

"Mr. Song swears Mr. West never took any, and we didn't find any at their house. So I'm sorry but we are now treating this as a possible homicide."

"Who would want to kill Billy?" The idea was incredible.

Sid's voice was a little dry. "Well, that's the first question."

Thinking *this is unbelievable*, I said, "When do you want to talk?"

"How's eleven?"

"I'll round up the others."

"Thanks."

Red and Lesley were already up; he was out in the prop shop, working on something for his next project, and she was doing some surface design on something for her next project. There really is no downtime when you're show people. You're either trying to get a job, prepping for a job, or doing the job.

Why did I do this, anyway? I wondered sometimes. I was the lucky one, having a full-time job in the industry. But of course, the answer was easy: when you get used to being rewarded for performing, it's really tough to give that up. Because, let's face it, nobody gets applause for a letter well typed. And nobody pays attention to who's voicing a cartoon character, or narrating a commercial. I'd been in the background for what felt like a very long time. Chasing my own projects had always been – if exhausting – therapeutic.

After telling the others that we'd be seeing the detective again for sure, I did a quick sweep of the house. I wanted to look like a professional, not a flake.

And on some level, I think I wanted to reflect well on Billy. Which reminded me, I needed to call my mom and Uncle Kyong. Those were probably the two most awful conversations of my life.

Once I pulled myself together, I took a shower and did my face and hair a little more – okay, a lot more – carefully than I would have on an ordinary Tuesday. I stared into my tiny closet for a few minutes before deciding on cream linen slacks and a sleeveless crocheted silk tunic that a friend had made. It was a vivid tangerine color, and always made me feel happier. I topped the tunic with a multi-strand bead necklace and matching earrings. Usually I didn't wear shoes around the house, but this was a different situation. My best option was a pair of Munro platform slides with a fake snakeskin finish. Being a few inches taller would help establish authority. I hoped.

The detective had been nothing but professional and respectful at the theater, even though I could tell he was surprised when he saw me. Everyone is. Nobody expects the short black girl to be in charge. Nobody expects 'Tanith Salazar' to be a short black girl. That was one reason I'd changed my name from Tabitha. (Did my mother have something to say about that? Yes, yes she did. But if you grew up being called Tabby you would have changed your name too.) The element of surprise had given me an advantage in numerous business situations. I thought it might have been an advantage yesterday, too. But now he knew what to expect.

One great benefit of being biracial is cool hair. Mine is black like you'd expect, but with a texture I would describe as Labradoodle. It's not tightly curly and it's soft in the hand. I was currently wearing it about shoulder-length, generally in a ponytail because it's easy. Today I took a couple of minutes to roll up the pony and pin it into a much sleeker shape than I usually bothered with.

Hey. I might have been wishing I had some Visine, but I could see just fine. And Detective Cutie was on his way over. By the time I was costumed and made up, I had found my character for the day. If I didn't think about Billy, I might even pull it off.

II. Ysidro

I left the theater that first night certain that I had no clue what had happened, or how (or whether) the show people were involved. I'd investigated showbiz people before but it was always obvious stuff – drugs or domestic issues or car accidents. This was a case of a person who seemed to be low on the suicide or homicide probability scale. But there it was, he was dead. I needed to talk to everyone else in the cast, and I needed to get my mind off Miss Tanith Salazar.

She'd told me she was Filipino and black. I was Filipino and Mexican. It had been a long time since someone had flipped my switch, and now was about the worst possible time. I was aware that I was – inappropriately – thinking of her by her first name, and had been right from the start. That hadn't happened before. I hoped I'd be able to keep it inside my head.

The next morning I checked in first thing for the tox results and knew we were in for it. I briefed my commander, then called up Mr. Song. He said we could come over again and take a closer look at the house. Washington and Muñoz came with me.

"I'd like you guys to come over to the Salazar place later too," I said. "I know there's some legwork to do, and we need to set up interviews with all the people we missed last night. But I want to talk to all three of those characters in one room and I need extra eyes and ears to make sure I don't miss something."

"Sure, can do," Muñoz said.

"If that oxycontin wasn't in the Song/West house," said Washington, "we've got a problem."

We all stared gloomily at each other. Tracing drugs was next to impossible. I hated to think this one might go cold because we couldn't establish who had access to the murder weapon.

The Salazar house-sharing arrangement was located on the northwest edge of Van Nuys, with a big rambling ranch house on a corner lot. Three cars crowded the driveway, and the yard had a set of wooden picnic furniture painted in bright colors. Up close I could see that it was actually lines from plays, in bright paint on white. The sources were in black letters. "Very educational furniture," I said, reading a quote from Shakespeare.

Muñoz said, "That must have taken days." Washington had his eyebrows up like he wasn't sure what we were in for. The last time we'd gone on an industry-related home interview, it had been at a pretentiously modern house. Could have belonged to a dentist for all the artistic expression on display. I had a feeling that was not what we were about to walk into.

The carport had canvas sides with vinyl 'windows,' and I assumed (after my talk with Warner) that this served as the prop shop. I was interested to see the inside.

Tanith greeted us at the door, composed and well-dressed and red-eyed and completely made up. I deduced a crying jag followed by repairs, and thought she looked gorgeous. She offered coffee or a tour. We opted for the tour. Warner and Hayes were there, hanging back.

I have to admit, my one-bedroom condo wasn't much to look at, and hadn't been since my last girlfriend moved out. My whole life happened at the station, or on the street. It was always interesting to me to see other people's living spaces. I was a little too interested in this one.

The main living area included a living room, dining room, and kitchen. Each room was painted in bright colors, and was furnished with what Tanith admitted were thrift-store finds – including the ten mismatched chairs in the dining room. But the rustic dining table had Warner's name carved along its edge. The flooring was Saltillo tile and there were colorful chandeliers. It looked like my Mexican grandma's idea of heaven, and smelled of cinnamon.

Sam wandered over to the biggest window and fingered the substantial drapery. "My wife would love this," he said.

"Lesley made those," said Tanith. "Cheap serapes from Tijuana, bleached and overdyed." Teresa nodded with comprehension and I tried to look like I knew what that meant.

Warner's room was sparely furnished. He had a high-quality computer system, a bookcase bench full of technical and art books, and a custom built platform bed. It wasn't an empty-looking room, though, thanks to the costume, armor, and weaponry displayed on the walls. "You make all this stuff?" I asked. He nodded. "How'd you learn to do all this?"

"There's a lot of downtime in this profession," he said. "I like to stay busy. I've had years when I did more work in props than anything else." It made sense, and I had to admire the guy; I'd met plenty of actors and most of them filled their time with day jobs that had to be pretty uninspiring. It looked as though this guy would rather stay in the groove at all times.

The creative vibe was just as obvious in Hayes' room. It was both colorful and well-organized. She had a 5x5 Ikea Expedit shelf in there, its cubes filled with rolls and stacks of fabrics. The opposite wall was covered with pegboard hung with stuff I couldn't identify, but which had Muñoz letting out a "Oooooh" that I would torture her about later. A daybed on the third wall faced a high-tech sewing machine flanked by Ikea drawer units, all squeezed between the closet door and the bedroom's entry door.

Tanith's room was the smallest of the three, mostly because the bed was fitted into three continuous walls of books. Built-in shelves started out eighteen inches deep and gradually got shallower going up. Even the closet door had books on it – paperbacks stacked inside shallow wooden boxes.

I read, don't get me wrong. Mostly nonfiction. That many books was almost scary. "Did Mr. Warner build these shelves for you?" I probably didn't need to ask.

Tanith looked at me like the answer should have been obvious, but said, "Yes, he did. The alternative was having books all over the house." This, of course, told me that while she might be collaborative, there were some things she did not negotiate.

On the inside wall, a small multi-level desk held an up-to-date PC setup, including a printer/scanner, a half-sized music keyboard, and a shelf loaded with a digital SLR camera and its accessories. That stuff, I felt comfortable with.

Warner also let us have a look at the prop shop. There were sturdy wooden cabinets bolted to the wall and the equipment he had in there would have made my dad, a hobby carpenter, drool. I gave him a sidelong glance. "You don't worry about this stuff getting stolen?"

"It's all insured. And we have ADT."

I shook my head, but the truth was that the hand tools were better-secured than my dad's had ever been. And it is not so easy for a petty thief to walk off with a radial arm saw.

As we went back in to the living room I felt like I understood them all much better. These were people who lived their work, in a way that I didn't often see. They also appeared to be serious, methodical, and professional about their work.

"Tanith Salazar, Drew Warner, and Lesley Hayes," I said after we were all seated. "How is it you came to this arrangement?"

"Ugh, call me Red please. Tanith and I were in college together. Then we met Lesley on a job about ten years ago and we got along."

Hayes said, "I had the chance to rent this place. The homeowner had just moved out, she was a parent of a friend, my friend had his own place and didn't want to move here, and they wanted to rent it because the income would help pay for the assisted living. But they were all like, no college students please. I couldn't swing it by myself, so I asked Tanith, and she suggested bringing in Red."

"It turned out great," said Warner. "People started hiring us as a group."

"We have complementary skill sets," said Tanith.

"Yeah, I guess so," I said. "So now that we've broken the ice, let me hit you with the tough question. The tox report indicates Mr. West ingested the drug between eight p.m. and midnight, almost certainly with that tea drink. He was at home all day before going downtown." The coffee shop where he bought the tea had security cameras that covered the prep station; the drink hadn't been tampered with there. "So do you know of anyone associated with the show who might have had access to oxycontin?"

There was a brief, uncomfortable silence. Then Hayes sighed. "It may have been mine."

"Lesley, what the hell," said Tanith.

"Remember when I had that back injury, and I did physical therapy, but they gave me that prescription. And I never used all of it because it made me all, like, cross-eyed."

"Is it still here?"

"Well, no. I checked this morning, and it's gone."

I cut in. "Where did you keep it?"

"It was in the bathroom medicine cabinet."

It was all I could do not to sigh. "Muñoz, could you go take a look at the bathroom please?" Teresa nodded and went down the hall. "Do you have any idea when someone might have had an opportunity to take it?"

Hayes said, "Actually yeah. Remember we had the cast party, Tanith? The meet and greet and read-through. Everybody was here, even the social dancers. People were in and out of the house all night."

"So this is everybody on the list you gave me?"

"Yeah, everybody. Even that one ballroom dancer who we gave the prompt/runner job to."

"Shit, that reminds me, we need someone to help with props," Tanith said. "Red?"

"Anthony already emailed me and volunteered."

"Who is Anthony again?" I said.

He said, "Roberts. One of the social dancers."

"Okay. So how long ago was this cast party, and was it the only time you can think of that everybody was here?"

"It was ..." I could see Tanith counting back in her head, "about four weeks ago. We'd already given the scripts and music to our singing parts but I wanted everybody to get the shape of the show in their heads. Because the rehearsals were going to be really broken up. We weren't going to have every single scene running until we got to the theater."

"And yeah, it was the only time everybody was here," Hayes said firmly. "We've had some tech-type meetings here, and the wardrobe consult, but I honestly don't think anybody went to my bathroom during those."

"Maybe." Warner looked thoughtful. "Yoshi and Valerie both used the main bathroom two weeks ago. I remember because Yoshi asked where some more tissue was and Valerie had a sneezing fit from the room freshener. But I wasn't here when the wardrobe consult was going on."

"So that's," I consulted my list, "the lighting guy and the music person."

"Right," said Tanith.

Muñoz came back in. "It's super clean in there."

"I'm a little OCD," Hayes said, as if she figured we would think that was a bad thing. I frankly didn't see how she could do what she did without a little OCD.

Warner shrugged. "We all are."

"Okay, so not much point getting a forensic team out here. We have some more people to talk to today. Before we go, I need to ask if any of you has any idea who, among your cast and crew, might have had some

29

reason to get Mr. West out of the way. Was he in anybody's way? Who could have profited, or benefited, from taking him out of the show? Who do you know least well? Is there anybody who's, you know, seemed sketchy about anything at any time. Give it some thought and contact me with any ideas you have."

There was a chorus of "Okay." I studied them all. Tanith looked upset again. Warner looked mad.

Hayes looked apologetic. "I knew I should have turned that shit back in to the pharmacy," she said. "I just thought, you know, if one of us got hurt again it might be handy to have around. And it was so expensive. I'm sorry."

"Whatever happened, I'm pretty sure it wasn't your fault," I said to her. I don't think she believed me.

Before we left, Tanith gave me printouts of the whole production schedule, the scene chart, and the script. "I don't know if this will be helpful to you or not," she said, "but with so many people to talk to I thought it couldn't hurt."

"No, this is great," I said. "Thanks for thinking of it. We'll be in touch."

Washington and Muñoz volunteered to call in as many of the cast and crew as possible to the station. "I think we can stuff them all in the main conference room," Teresa said. "And keep them under observation while we talk to one at a time."

"Somebody has to have seen something," said Sam. "Whether at this party or at the theater. And people will be speculating."

"If they're all crammed in there, they're going to talk. Something will bubble up."

"Fine by me," I said. "Let me know who you can't get in between one and five today. We have to go off the clock by then, so if there's anyone we have to go to, I'd like to try and squeeze it in by end of shift."

"Yeah, wish the department wasn't so tight on overtime." Sam gave me a sympathetic look.

"I already got my ass handed to me for yesterday." Just one of those things. We couldn't really have put off the trip downtown; it was the only place we knew to find all these people. Getting chewed out about it was on my to-do list as soon as I'd spoken to Mr. Song.

"That visit to the theater was helpful, though. I've never been backstage in one before," said Teresa.

"The map you guys made is great. Did you get a sense of where the cast members spent most of their time on the Sunday?"

Sam said, "Yeah, definitely in the dressing room and the holding area. It didn't look like anyone had even been upstairs."

"I didn't go up there," I said. "Pretty empty?"

"Nothing," said Teresa. "Jackson said they aren't using the dressing rooms upstairs. The cast members were mostly sitting in the audience seats when they weren't onstage Sunday. By the way, that catwalk is a horror show."

"So I heard. Thanks for going up there. I'm not seeing that anybody had special interactions with West aside from Miz Salazar."

"We could push on that," said Sam. "Time-wise, it looks like the theater's where the oxy got into the tea. So somebody had some issue with him."

"Talking to Salazar and company this morning was helpful too," Teresa said. "They're pretty tight, huh."

31

"According to Miz Hayes," I said, "Warner and Salazar had a thing before they all moved in together."

"But not anymore," Sam said. It wasn't a question.

"Nope."

"Wonder where he's getting it?"

"Jeez, Sam," said Teresa. "Don't be such a guy."

"Well, you gotta wonder. Guy like that, living with two women; one's an ex and one is otherwise inclined. Is that camouflage or what?"

"It's something to remember, but I don't think further investigation is called for at this time," I said gently, and suggested it was time to set up the interviews.

As it turned out, Sam and Teresa were able to call in all but six of the company members. I found out all but one of those six were on the west side, and arranged a string of workplace and home visits to knock out the interviews. I'd be seeing four of the social dancers – who I didn't expect to have much to do with the case – a person whose part was 'Girl,' and a guy Tanith had said I should talk to, who was cast as 'Henchman.'

And boy, did he look the part. He was about six-four and broad as a bus. "Marco Hidalgo, hi. My colleague took your statement last night, but you may have heard we have some new information. So besides talking about your experience at the theater on Sunday, I need to ask you a few questions about the audition process and the other rehearsals you've been to. Oh, and I understand there was a sort of cast party a few weeks back. Were you there?"

"Yes, we were all there," he said quietly. He sounded like James Earl Jones. "I was really excited. Because of getting the Henchman part, but also because I was understudying Mr. West."

"Were you acquainted with Mr. West?"

"I worked on a movie with him. I was an extra and he had a small speaking part."

"So had you done this kind of project before?"

"Never a stage project, not since coming to L.A. I went to a good theater school but I never got to do much there, either, because of how I look."

I gave him my best sympathetic expression. "Tell me how the understudy thing works."

"Well, my part only has a few lines. The parts Mr. West was playing were small roles too – a cop, and a waiter – but he was understudying Victor himself. I learned the lines and the business for the cop and the waiter, Mr. West learned Victor's whole part. That's Victor Garcia, he plays the villain, the Ivory part."

I nodded. I knew that already, of course, but he was trying to be helpful. "Business, that's the stuff you do onstage, right?"

"Right, like where to enter, where to exit, where your marks are, how to react to other actors, if you're handling any props."

I checked my notes. "You and Mr. West and Mr. Garcia, you're all very different physical types. Mr. West was old enough to be your father."

"He was the Grand Old Man of the cast," Hidalgo said with a faint smile. "He's done it all. Just for fun one time, he did a couple of the Ivory scenes. It was spooky as shit."

"Tell me about it."

"Well, so Victor, he's kind of slinky and sexy in the part, you know? Seductive. Mr. West played it like the friendly uncle. Only the friendly uncle who takes porno pictures of his niece."

"Nice."

"It would have completely changed the show. I got it on video if you want to see."

I did, actually; I hadn't had time to look up West and see how he'd been in life. So Hidalgo got out his phone and played it for me. West was not only giving some lines, he was singing one of the songs. He looked and sounded a little like Kevin Spacey, and yeah, it was spooky as shit. "So now you're understudying that part too."

"God, I know. I mean, I know the songs, but I never expected to be called on to do it. I still don't. I'm not sure how I would play it."

"Whereas a cop and a waiter aren't too complicated?" My voice might have been a little dry. Thanks to all the cop shows, everybody thinks they know what a cop is like.

"Yeah."

"Okay. So Mr. Warner, he was the fill-in for Mr. West. Now he's taking those parts and understudying Ivory. What happens if a light bar falls on his head?"

"Oh God, don't even joke about it!"

I let him sit with it a moment. "Well?"

Hidalgo looked at me uncertainly. "I guess I'd take the cop and waiter parts."

"And then what happens if something happens to Victor Garcia? Wouldn't you get the Ivory part?"

He looked scared now. "Whoa, wait a second."

"You never thought about that?"

"No! I mean, well. Okay. For a minute. Like you do, you know. What if. But I don't want that. I really don't. I'm not ready for that."

"Don't you want to be a star?"

"Sure. Who doesn't? But I see Victor play it and I know I'm not there yet. I don't want to get a big break like that until I know I won't fuck it up. And I sure wouldn't want to get it because somebody else got hurt."

"Okay. So moving on." By the end of the interview I had learned some interesting things. Like: Hidalgo got very nervous when I talked about this person playing the Girl. I pushed a little here and there. But I had to get to the next rendezvous, so I told him, in my best nice-cop voice, that I might want to talk to him again, and I moved on.

As expected, the social dancers weren't good for much. They were all so giggle-headed over being in a show, and so focused on where they needed to be and what they needed to be doing, that most of them hadn't noticed where anyone was at the theater at any given time. One of the women did give me something, though: she'd seen this same person, the one playing the Girl, coming out of the back bathroom at the Salazar house.

The Girl's name was Susan Redding, and she was last on my list. When I asked her about it, she said, "Um, honestly, it was a girl thing. I went to that bathroom because I was hoping to find a tampon. And I did."

That was hard to argue with, it was the kind of personal detail that a lot of people would have skated around, but it gave me a little tingle. Anytime someone says "honestly" I assume they are lying. So I filed it away. It's tough being such a cynic, but I've been a cop for fourteen years. And let me tell you, people lie.

I wrote up the notes from all those interviews, logged the recordings, and wondered who else was lying. Some of these people had been actors for a long time.

III. Tanith

After the cops were gone I sat for a while thinking about what might have happened, and how it might have happened. It seemed clear to me that Sid - Detective Palacio – I probably should be thinking of him with his rank – thought someone had stolen Lesley's oxycontin and kept it for a rainy day. And then decided that Billy was raining on his (or her) parade. But I couldn't for the life of me imagine who it could be.

It was inconceivable to me that Red would ever do anything to damage a show, much less my show. But Red was the swing for those two parts. And he was the one who'd get moved up to Ivory if, gods forbid, something happened to Victor.

That thought just about made me break out in a rash. I texted Victor: *Do me a favor and stay away from the rest of the cast till 2nd tech.* After an hour or so I got a text back: *No problem. I hate all those fuckers anyway. LOL*

I knew he was kidding. Victor was a pussycat.

Which reminded me. I needed an excuse to get out of the house, and the theater cat seemed like a good one. What if he starved before Wednesday night? I'd never forgive myself.

Of course, getting downtown was a project, and then finding parking was a nightmare. But toward late afternoon I was walking down the alley behind the theater, and there was the cat, perched on the fire escape above.

"How did you get up there?" I asked. He blinked down at me. I surveyed the back of the building and deduced that the cat had made an approximately six-foot leap from the top of a dumpster. I looked back at him with respect. "Do you want something to eat, or are you full of pigeon Cordon Bleu?" Proving my theory, the cat jumped from the fire escape platform to the dumpster, then to the ground, and moseyed over to me.

"You may have to come home with me after this show," I said softly, setting down some food and water for him. He really didn't look like he needed it: this was one prosperous alley cat. But something about him charmed me. Maybe it was the alternating black and white toes on his hind feet, or maybe it was that one of his balls was black and the other one was orange. We weren't supposed to have a cat; Red was allergic, and Lesley had that fabric situation. But I couldn't quite see leaving this guy in the alley. Maybe Red could build him a cat house.

I leaned against the wall of the building, thinking ridiculous thoughts like that. The cat may not have been super hungry, but he also wasn't the kind of guy who would say no to free food. He cleaned his plate and then sat down and washed his face. I took his picture with my phone, planning to post it on the Kickstarter project page.

"I shouldn't even be here, Mr. Cat," I said. "I have to go home now and make sure my show doesn't fall apart. See you tomorrow."

He blinked at me. I reached down to pet his head and he hooked a paw over my wrist. No claws, just the paw. We stared into each other's eyes for a minute.

"You are spooky, Mr. Cat. Are you trying to tell me something? Who doctored Billy's tea, Mr. Cat?"

Of course, he couldn't really tell me. I wished he could.

Back at home, I checked my email and found another round of cast questions to answer. While I was doing that, a call came in from the detective. After indulging an initial burst of resentment and anxiety, I took a breath and called him back. "What can I do for you, Detective?"

"Sorry to bother you, Miz Salazar, but a couple of questions came up. Can you confirm for me which rehearsals your social dancers were called for ... am I getting that right?"

"Yes," I said. "After the casting was done, we had a couple of weeks of doing contracts, production design, and readings with the leads. After that was the cast party, when everybody came here. The next week was the wardrobe consult. The week after that, we did a full cast reading and blocking of all the club scenes. Then the following weekend, we did all those scenes with just the dancers. Then this past weekend we did a rehearsal strictly for all the dancers. That was Saturday."

"So the social dancers were called ... five times, including the party and the wardrobe thing, before Sunday's read-through?"

"Right."

"None of the amateur dancers had any lines, is that right?"

"Right. They are all background to the main action; they're onstage to give the set the look of a real bar or dance hall. I basically told them to dance if they felt like dancing, mime some other interactions, stay out of the real actors' way, applaud the featured dancers and singers, and otherwise don't make a sound."

"How were they doing?"

"They got a little excited this Sunday when we got to the theater."

"Any sign any of them was unhappy with the arrangement, or wanted more to do?"

Good grief, I thought. "No, nothing like that."

"Okay, so could you tell me about the wardrobe thing?"

"Everybody was providing as much of their own stuff as possible, but the production filled in the gaps. People came in with what they had, and Lesley went over their costume requirements to see what else might be needed."

"Was there a particular time people were coming?"

"No, it was a drop-in thing. Lesley was here all day, so people came when they could."

"Was there anyone who did not come for a wardrobe consult?"

I flipped through my notes. "Um ... actually yes. Miranda, our featured singer, sent an email with photos of the dresses she was proposing to wear. Lily, our stripper, did the same thing with her costume. They both had out-of-town stuff happening that day."

"Anybody else?"

"Marco, the Henchman, basically has one costume which is a plain black suit. Marco came to the audition wearing that and we let him know it was fine to use it. Dexter Parker, who plays a customer and a waiter, also came to audition in a suit which would work for his appearances. It was a three-piece, so he could wear it three different ways, and then just throw on an apron as the waiter. And Billy."

"Mr. West didn't come to the consult?"

"He was an actor longer than I've been alive. For playing a plainclothes cop and a waiter, I wouldn't have dared to micromanage him."

"Okay, I'll let you go now. Thank you very much, Miz Salazar."

"Call me Tanith."

"Tanith." I heard a smile in his voice. "Oh, one more thing."

And here I thought Columbo was fictitious. "What's that?"

"How many people auditioned who were not cast?"

"Ay caramba. Uh ... fewer than twenty. I have that information somewhere. You don't need to talk to all of those people too, do you?"

"I don't think so, but I'll let you know. Thanks."

"You're welcome." I hung up. It took me a few minutes to settle down after that conversation. It was starting to sink in that one of my cast was probably responsible for what happened to Billy. It was a horrible thought.

Red and Lesley and I had a conference over dinner. The reality was, if nothing else happened, and the cops didn't shut us down, we were still good to go. Billy had taken his parts as a favor to me, and I knew Red would be fine. He worked behind the scenes more than on stage because of his looks, not because of his talent. Kind of like me.

"Do you think we all do what we do because we have something to prove?" I asked after dinner, while we were polishing off a cheap bottle of wine. Okay, a second cheap bottle.

"Well sure," said Lesley. "I mean, obviously."

"No doubt," said Red. "I should have Brad Pitt's career. But I don't look like Brad Pitt."

"You're too tall," said Lesley. "All the big Hollywood stars are short."

"Not as short as they used to be," I said, laughing.

"But none of them look like an actual Viking."

"That is true."

Red nodded owlishly. "Even that dude playing Thor. I'd like to see him handle a claymore."

I would too, the wine and I thought. Actually I'd like to see Thor and Red face off. Same height, same general hunk factor, we could make a fortune with that show. Among his many other gigs, Red played a knight at Renaissance fairs. He was awfully good at it. There's a lot to be said for a man with a long sword. I put my hand on his arm. "I promise my next play will be a sword-and-sorcery story."

"Yeah, why'd you want to do this Eighties noir thing anyway?" Lesley upended the bottle and looked disappointed when nothing came out.

I giggled at her expression, which set Red off. Eventually I remembered the question. "Well, I wrote the treatment when I was wallowing in a bad breakup and reading everything by Andrew Vachss."

"Who is who."

"He was a lawyer specializing in child sexual abuse prosecutions and boy, was he mad about it. He wrote this whole series about a vigilante. The first treatment I wrote was pitch black. It was very therapeutic."

"Did you write your ex into it?"

"Well sure. He got knifed in the first act."

They both hooted. Red said, "Jeez, remind me not to break up with any writers."

I thumped him. "You already did." It had been more a mutual eh-this-isn't-really-working thing than a breakup, to be fair. At least I'd thought it was, at the time. Since then we'd had enough late-night talks with enough wine that I knew better. But we still played it as if he broke up with me for the usual reasons. It was good for his ego.

He was giving me that look, that 'thanks for rewriting the story' look. "That was a million years ago, and I didn't even know you were writing then."

"I wasn't," I admitted. I'd been headed to graduate school, picking up acting jobs whenever and wherever I could, and hardly had time to think, much less write.

Then Lesley asked, "When did this thing turn into a musical?"

This was fun. We'd been talking about the project all year, but never about my process of writing it. It was like, they knew I was a weirdo who was always scribbling something, but they were basically working on it because I asked them to. (And, let's face it, because I could pay them.)

I said, "I dated a guy who wrote pop songs and he was kind of snotty about it, so I did a throwdown. I bet him I could write a pop ballad in two hours or less. And I did, and needless to say he did not call me ever again."

Lesley bellowed with laughter. "This is why I date women. The egos are not so fragile."

"Maybe not about work," Red muttered.

"But yeah, after that I started thinking about the play again and wondered if I could do it as a musical. So it was kind of a challenge to myself."

"You're an overachiever," said Lesley.

"No, I'm an insomniac." For a second there I thought, God! Writing a pop song? For someone who's studied music for decades, it's not exactly hard.

And then we all looked at each other, and the big question was hanging in the middle of the room so heavily you could practically see it. We all kind of hastily made our excuses, cleaned up the dinner stuff, and went to our rooms. I was feeling much too sober now.

I took another slug of Zzz-Quil. At that moment, I didn't care whether it was true that it wasn't habit-forming.

III. Ysidro

I got back to the station in time to do a little off-the-clock review with Washington and Muñoz. They had some interesting notes for me from all those interviews, but nothing quite as tingly as what I'd gotten from Hidalgo and Redding.

"The only person who seemed a little off to me was this Waiter 2 dude, Dexter Parker," said Sam. "A few people said he seemed to be everywhere."

"We got two Parkers, don't we? No relation, I assume," I said. Miranda was blonde and Dexter was black.

"No relation," said Sam with a smile.

"But someone else said they thought he had a thing for Miz Salazar," said Teresa. "Would someone mess up a cast when they were crushing on the director? I mean, that wouldn't do much good, would it?"

"I can't imagine how," I agreed. "Still, we should follow up. Anybody else?"

"This Victor Garcia seemed a little more upset than I would have expected," said Teresa. "I asked him if he and West had worked together before, he said no. I asked if they knew each other socially, he said no. So then I said he seemed kind of rocky, and he said they'd gotten friendly since the show started."

"How friendly? Is this Garcia gay?"

"I think so."

"Did you push it?"

"Yeah, I pushed it," she said, irritated. "He said they'd been talking during the rehearsals and were both looking at a project that's casting next week. Garcia said he hoped they'd be working together."

"So possibly just a work connection, but possibly also the start of something else. We're going to need to talk to Garcia again, and ask a few people how West's marriage really was. Sometimes getting married can flip a long-term cohab on its head."

"And Garcia's pretty much a fox," said Teresa.

"I can follow up with Garcia," said Sam, giving her a look. "And then Mr. Song."

I nodded and made a note. "Okay, so anything else? Any obvious lies?"

"I think everybody may have exaggerated how punctual they were," said Sam. "I mean, people don't generally make a note of the exact time they do things. Otherwise, not obviously."

Teresa nodded. "It's a small cast. It doesn't really work out good for anybody if the show gets damaged. Especially not the crew people. I think we can move them all to the bottom of the list."

I had to agree with Teresa on that too. From what I was beginning to understand, the people technically producing a show had as much on the line as the actors did. None of them had any backup at all. They were a tight group, and had circled their wagons long ago.

"My take is the crew group hasn't interacted much with the on-stage group," I suggested. "Except the wardrobe gal."

"Got the same thing," said Sam. Teresa nodded. "They're all friendly enough, but the music person doesn't want the cast asking her questions, and the lighting guy doesn't want cast members making suggestions. The sound guy doesn't want to talk to anybody. Everything goes through Jackson first, then Salazar."

"Says here she's thirty-five," Teresa said. "Looks about eighteen."

"That's the Filipino genes," I said. "I'll still look fresh when you people are all grizzled."

"Bite me," Teresa invited. Sam laughed, and we broke it up. I took all their reports and went home to put in another couple of hours.

I read through everything again, and cleaned up my notes. Then I did a report for my commander so I wouldn't have to do it first thing in the morning (and while all the details were at the front of my memory). I knew what I thought had happened. But I didn't know why, and I wasn't sure how, and I wasn't positive about who. And I definitely had no clue if it might go any farther, or how we were going to prove it.

Every single person associated with the show had been at the theater Sunday afternoon and evening. Any one of them could have had the opportunity to doctor the tea. Three or four of them might be said to have an 'All About Eve' kind of motive. I didn't think much of it as a motive, but it was there.

My big problem with it was that the person who would be most likely to benefit was the person I thought least likely to interfere with the show.

Warner could say they were merely friends, but I could tell he cared about Tanith. Not just in the she's-my-roommate or she's-my-boss way, either. Lesley Hayes had confirmed there was a lot more than just a discussion in their history. Aside from the links of profession and personality, there couldn't be a much odder couple ... and I needed to quit speculating. For the investigation, what was important was that Tanith and Warner had both lied about that.

But I didn't think they had lied about anything else. They wanted the show to go on, so they wanted to sort this out, and if I pushed them, I was positive they would come clean on the relationship. I needed to find the other lies. Because while we had one witness saying they had seen someone coming from the bathroom where the drug had been kept, that didn't mean others hadn't been back there, others who hadn't been seen.

In other words, if you looked at the big picture it didn't look like we'd accomplished much. But if you've done this for a while, and you've got any kind of feel for it, you start to trust that tingle.

If the oxycontin tea cocktail had been an impulse or an experiment, nothing else might happen. On the other hand, if someone had a serious agenda, there were a couple other people who needed to watch their backs.

I studied the schedule Tanith had given me. They were due back in the theater the next night. There was no way I was going to get overtime approved, but there was also no law that said I couldn't show up there on my own time. It might actually help me figure this thing out if I watched the show.

Well, it was a good rationalization, right? It was a great chance to see how they all behaved in context.

Looking over the schedule I was struck by how detailed it was. I wondered if this was an updated version, if maybe they'd gone into it before everything was so tight, or if this was just how Tanith worked.

They'd done their main casting in one location and their amateur casting in another. The tech meetings had happened in several different places – mostly home offices and home studios. There'd been a legal meeting (labeled 'contracts') at an attorney's office, with a union rep present. There'd been the wardrobe consult and a production design meeting. And the cast party, of course.

Plus there were more than a dozen rehearsals, for various portions of the cast, at the Brewery, a dance studio, or a classroom. I was hoping we weren't going to have to verify with every person involved where they'd been on each of these dates.

Because the who was going to depend on the why, and I wasn't yet seeing how we could pin down the why until we knew pretty much everything about where and when.

I realized that the lamp on my entry table had gone out. It's on a timer; it was after midnight. Time to call it a day.

IV. Tanith

I slept late Wednesday morning, for which I thanked wine and Zzz-Quil, and woke up starving. I shuffled out to the kitchen in my robe like a slob, and rummaged around looking for food. It was a Mother Hubbard moment. We had one egg, some rice, and a package of Pop-Tarts. "This is ridiculous," I muttered as Lesley came in. She was looking all bright-eyed and holding a Starbucks cup. "Where did you get that?"

"Duh, at Starbucks. I've been up for hours. Red's all set with costume. Kevin checked in, he's contacted everyone who's on the call sheet for tonight."

"Great. You know, I think I'm going out for breakfast."

"Can I come?"

"I thought you'd been up for hours."

"That doesn't mean I had breakfast."

I had to concede that was true. I threw on a bright yellow broomstick skirt and a tie-dyed tee. It was already eighty-five degrees; September in the Valley, ugh. "Is Red around?"

"He took off after we finished his costume. I think he's got choreo today, for the Halloween thing."

Just as well. He probably would have conned me into buying his breakfast, like Lesley did. While we were waiting for the check, my phone buzzed. I dug it out of my bag to find a text from Marco. *Just want to confirm I'm called tonight.* I wrote back *Yes thanks for checking 7:00.* Then he sent a reply *Should Susan come*, and I didn't answer right away because I was thinking, why are you asking that?

"Lesley, check this out. Marco just asked if Susan should come to the theater tonight."

"Why does he care?"

"That's what I'm wondering." It pinged my radar, but I wrote back *No we don't need Susan till tomorrow. See you tonight*. Then Lesley and I stared at each other for a minute. Susan's part was the least demanding in the whole cast – one of our social dancers could have done it, if any of them had been young enough. It was little more than a walk-on. But she was the understudy for my ingénue.

Now, the ingénue was also not a huge part in terms of lines or stage business (which was why Susan wasn't called that night), but there were three songs. I didn't see how Marco's query might relate to what had happened to Billy, but anything even slightly off seemed automatically suspicious because of what had happened.

I was running out of other hands to be on. I thought I might mention this exchange to Sid.

"You know," said Lesley, on our way back to the house, "it seems like I do remember Marco and Susan being kind of handsy on Sunday. Maybe they have a thing going."

"Gaaahh," I said. "I don't care if people screw around, but if she's trying to sleep her way to the top she should have started with Brad." My show was Marco's first theater gig in L.A. Brad was our sound guy, and he was very connected. He was also fifty, potbellied, and balding.

"Or Valerie," said Lesley, and giggled.

"Hands off Valerie," I said. "She's happily married."

"Hey, just because the shop is closed that don't mean I can't look in the window."

I laughed, and we went off on a riff about fuckable co-workers until we got home. Then I called Sid. He picked up right away; my timing must have been good. "Good morning," he said. "How are you holding up?"

"I'm okay, thanks for asking. Listen, something a little strange happened this morning. I don't want to waste your time with trivia but, you did say anything sketchy."

"I meant it. So?"

"So I got a text from Marco, my Henchman, about tonight's tech rehearsal, and then a follow-up asking if Susan should be there. And I just thought, why would he be asking that. And then Lesley said she thought they might have a thing going."

"Hmm, that is interesting. Thanks for telling me."

"So there's no problem about tonight's rehearsal, right?"

"No problem. Go ahead as scheduled. If it's okay with you, I'd like to stop by the theater."

"Oh," I said, surprised. "Well, sure. Tech rehearsals are usually closed but it's not like you're press or something."

"If you want I can get my contact on the crime beat to show up." There was a smile in his voice again.

"No, thanks, that's okay. We're holding out for somebody from the entertainment pages."

He laughed. "Hey, while I've got you on the line, what can you tell me about Victor Garcia's relationship with Mr. West?"

"His what? As far as I know they didn't have a relationship."

"Detective Muñoz re-interviewed him yesterday and he said they were getting friendly. Wondered if you had any impressions."

"I didn't see anything beyond the professional," I said. "But ... ."

"Something come to mind?"

"Camille Monaghan – she's a teacher at the school where we did some rehearsals, Cameron's mom, my friend – she told me she'd noticed Victor and Billy talking during the breaks. Said they seemed kind of intense."

"When did you hear this?"

"Monday."

"So you haven't had a chance to speak with Mr. Garcia about it."

"I'm not sure that I would have," I lied.

"Can you give me Miz Monaghan's number?"

I'm pretty sure my voice sounded a little grouchy as I gave it to him. And I might not have been perfectly friendly when we said our goodbyes. It was inconceivable to me that Victor would have done anything to hurt Billy, and if the cops interfered with my villain I was well and truly fucked. I mean, Red could take the part, but Victor and Tony and Jenny and Cameron had their shit down. It's never a single part that's affected by a cast change.

The hours till seven seemed really long. I had taken two weeks' vacation to make sure I didn't have any work conflicts during the show weeks, but I wasn't used to having nothing to do. There was administrative stuff all the time, but the bulk of my work as writer and producer and director was either done (to the extent it could ever be called done) or would only be happening in the theater.

I couldn't mess around with the script because everyone knew their lines. I couldn't mess around with the songs because Valerie had already done the arrangements. My choreographer Alicia was out of town and would kill me if she found out after the fact that I'd touched her routines. I didn't want to even talk to my actors because I knew we would speculate and worry. So all I had to do, really, was hang around the house and obsess.

This is not such a great way to spend a day.

I did some obsessing anyway, thinking about the rehearsal schedule and the casting and when anyone could have had occasion to decide that getting rid of Billy might be a good thing. It seemed so ... pointless. Was it just because he made it easy, with his chai all the time?

It couldn't have been about his two small parts. But if it was about getting someone else into the Ivory part, why even look crosswise at Billy? Why not go straight for Victor? Did someone just want to create more opportunity, more possibility?

And then I circled back to, what the hell was this thing with Victor? I really didn't like the inference I was drawing, that the cops thought Victor and Billy might have had something going. I'd rather think of any other solution.

Despite what I'd told the detective, it was always possible that someone who hadn't been cast had a grudge against the production. It takes a certain amount of crazy to try to make it as an actor, and I would be the first to admit it. But the specific target was just plain wrong.

It was stupid. It was the act of someone who didn't understand how the theater worked. So I circled back to it being one of the newcomers or non-professionals.

Finally, fed up with myself, I decided to go grocery shopping. I might not be able to fix anything else, but at least I could make sure there was food in the house.

IV. Ysidro

After Tanith's call I decided to poke some people a little. Washington and Muñoz were working another case that day and I was swabbing the decks after something we'd closed the week before. It left me some time to think.

I spent a little too much time thinking about Tanith. Then I got busy on the phone. First I called Camille Monaghan, and was lucky enough to get her on the first try. She helpfully confirmed the conversation with Tanith, providing some detail on the Garcia-West encounters.

"Did it seem to you that their discussion was professional in nature?" I asked.

"I couldn't say," she said. "I don't know if you know a lot of gay men, but their body language tends to be more intimate than straight men. Even when they're just talking about the weather."

I actually had several gay friends, and she was right. "So you weren't able to overhear what they were saying."

"No, I was hanging out with my daughter on the other side of the room."

"Okay. We may need to speak with you again, but thanks for now."

"Oh, and Detective?" Her voice sounded cautious. "Yes?"

"Victor's not out. If it's possible to be discreet I know he would appreciate it."

"Yes ma'am, we'll do what we can." That was interesting too. When we'd asked about relationship status, Garcia had just said he was single. We hadn't spoken with anyone associated with the TV show he worked on, and I could count on Washington and Muñoz not to gossip. As far as I knew, no one else in the cast had made any reference to Garcia's private life. Which meant either he was super discreet himself, or everyone liked him and didn't want to mess with him, or both. It didn't mean anything for the investigation, necessarily, but it was the kind of character note that can help an investigator when he's assessing statements.

I wrote up the conversation with Ms. Monaghan, and then dialed again. "So hey, Mr. Hidalgo. Detective Palacio here."

"Uh, good morning. What can I do for you?"

"I just wanted to clarify something. Was there anyone in the cast or crew, aside from Mr. West, who you'd worked with previously?"

"No."

"Anyone you'd seen in a live performance before?"

"I'd seen Lily. She plays Crystal, the stripper."

"None of the ballroom dancers?"

"No."

"Okay, so is there anybody you've been spending more time with since the process started?"

"Uh, what?"

The stalling, the suddenly higher pitch of his voice, I loved that. "Well, you've been at the initial casting call, the callback, the first reading, the cast party with the read-through, and two Saturday rehearsals where they did all the club scenes, is that right?"

"Yes, last Saturday was just what Tanith called crowd scenes. The showgirls, the pro dancers, and all the amateur dancers."

"Okay, and then the theater run-through. You were with some of these people a lot. There wasn't anybody you got friendly with?"

"Well, we all got friendly. It's a nice bunch of people."

"Come on, Marco. There's a bunch of pretty women in this show." Starting at the top, I couldn't help thinking.

"I, um, okay. I went out for coffee once with Liz and Lily and Miranda."

"How about Miss Redding?"

There was a really pregnant pause, then I heard a little giving-in sigh. "We might have gotten a bite to eat once or twice."

"Well, which is it – once or twice?"

"Okay, we went out after both the scene rehearsals. Those were daytime ... we were all done by six."

"Any other time?"

"I went to the Brewery last Friday night, when Tanith was running the songs. I wanted to hear the songs," he clarified, unnecessarily.

"And Miss Redding was there because she's, let me see, Miss Monaghan's understudy."

"Right."

"Thanks very much, Marco. That's helpful. Have a good day." I disconnected and thought, Hayes was right. I was all warmed up now, so I called Susan Redding.

She sounded pissy. "Do we really have to do this again?"

Oh, yes we do, I thought, and gave her my bored-but-irritated voice. "If it's an inconvenient time maybe you'd like to come in to the station later."

"No, it's just – I mean, it's okay. Whatever."

So I asked her the same questions as I'd asked Hidalgo, and got parallel responses, served up with a side of attitude. Except she said Hidalgo had been at both the Friday rehearsals at the Brewery, just hanging out. See? People lie.

"Where was Mr. Hidalgo during those rehearsals?"

"He just hung out, outside. He knew if he came in they would have to pay him or else make sure he left, so he stayed out of sight." There was a note of contempt in her voice.

Then I asked, "What are you doing tonight?"

"What do you mean?"

"Well, there's a tech rehearsal, right? What do you do when the show is working but you're not called?"

"I work on my own stuff. I've got my own stuff."

"What brought you to Hollywood?"

"I auditioned for American Idol and almost got on. My parents said I could spend a year out here trying to break in."

"This your first theater job?"

"No," she said scornfully. "I've done a bunch of stuff."

"And you have a day job. Sorry, I should have asked – are you at work?"

"I'm going in later," she said grudgingly.

"Okay. Thanks a lot." I disconnected and thought, there is more to get out of that one. I ran a quick Google search; 'almost got on' translated to 'cut at the city tryouts.' She did have an IMDB page, and there were a couple of music videos listed. An attached resumé listed high school and community theater work. Otherwise all that was online was a slew of overtly sexy photographs.

I had the feeling Miss Susan was one of those who are told, by everybody at home in the small town, how great they are, and can't understand why they don't get any traction in the big city.

There are a lot of those. It's easy to be the best singer or dancer in a small town. But when every waiter and every barista seems to have a head shot, it's not so easy to get noticed. I wondered why Tanith had cast her, specifically. Since I had come up with a few other questions, I made another call. She answered, "You again?" and I thought, Ouch. After first ascertaining that she had time and was at least nominally willing to talk, I cut to the chase.

"Wondering why you chose to cast Susan Redding."

"Needed a young singer who could look blank and would work for a non-union show. She's not a great singer, but the odds of losing Cameron were low."

"You've worked with Miss Monaghan before?"

"No, but she's the daughter of my friend Camille."

"Oh right, you mentioned that."

"Well, she did a genuine audition; there were six girls who tried for that role, including Susan." Tanith sounded a little defensive.

"Okay, thanks. Now, I was looking at this scene chart and you have this note about the swing roles. The male parts have what I'd call plenty of coverage, but Cassandra is doubled by your singer and then nobody."

"If Jenny or Miranda had to drop out, I know about three dozen qualified singer-actresses who I could beg, borrow, or bribe. Or I figured I could fill in myself in a pinch."

"So that explains that. Then I had another question."

"Okay." Slight impatience, but a note of curiosity.

"How did your financing thing work?"

"Why do you ask?"

"You never know what might be relevant."

She sighed. "We did a Kickstarter. Everybody who contributed at least a hundred dollars gets a ticket to the show, two hundred gets two tickets, five hundred gets two tickets to opening night plus their names in the program. Unless they opted out. Some people don't want other people to know they give money away."

"I can imagine. Did you put any of your own money in?"

"I was prepared to finance the whole thing myself, but as it turned out we got a good response. Mom put in, and her boss. Uncle Billy and Uncle Kyong."

"Is this a thing where the investors get paid back?"

"There's no financial reward. We're filming the dress rehearsal and everybody gets a copy of that. Also, our backing exceeded our request, so we're having a catered wrap party closing night, with all our backers invited."

"So, to clarify, the only benefit your investors get is if the show actually goes on."

"Right. Wow."

I could tell the penny had dropped. "Okay, thanks. Circling back to the casting. How did that work?"

"I placed ads in the trades and gave the info to Mom to spread around her casting contacts. Do you need to know how it broke out?"

"If it's not too much trouble." I heard her flipping through her notes.

"Seven professional ballroom dancers came. From those I cast Felipe and Liz. Liz has stage and commercial experience, Felipe's just a really phenomenal dancer. The showgirls all came as a group, they're part of a bigger group that performs regularly at a club in Hollywood. I didn't see anybody else for the showgirls. I had six actor/singers read for Evan, Ivory, Mickey, and the Henchman."

"So there were only two who read who weren't cast for something?"

"Right. Dexter read, I already knew him, and I cast him for the non-speaking customer/waiter part and as a swing for Felipe because I knew he could dance. He's also understudying the Henchman. And I asked Billy personally to play Mickey."

"I'd like to check out the gentlemen who weren't cast. Can you send me their contact information?"

"Sure."

"Then how about the women?"

"I think I told you six girls read for Fox. Four of those weren't cast. Two were underage, and two just weren't right for it. I hand-picked Lily – I've worked with her before. Seven women read for Cassandra, including Miranda. And thirteen amateur dancers came."

"Great. Um ... was it always your intention to cast the singer and the girl the way you did?"

"I was hoping it would work out that those parts could serve as understudies. The fewer people on the payroll, the better; and everyone has more fun when they are guaranteed to have something to do. Miranda has a great presence as a lounge singer, and she's actually more of a singer than an actress. So she was happy to get the part with two solos. Cassandra doesn't have a solo."

"Thanks for giving me so much of your time. I think – oh, one more thing."

"Yes, Detective Columbo?"

I laughed, couldn't help it. "Who's this Dexter Parker? You gave him a lot to do."

"He's got range. I needed a certain number of bodies, and between the two of them Marco's physical type had Henchman written all over it, so that's how I cast it. But I guess I think of Dexter as a utility player."

"He's somebody you've known?"

"In what sense?"

"I heard he might have a little bit of a thing for you."

She sighed. "We met on a project several years ago, and yeah, there's a crush. He's harmless though. He's actually a sweet guy."

"Just no spark, huh?"

"Not for me. Um ... do you ask these kinds of questions all the time?"

"No." I'd let her puzzle that one out. "See you later."

By the time I finished writing all that up, Washington and Muñoz had gotten back and were getting their reports in. "You guys want to grab a burger after shift?" I said.

"In-n-Out?" Sam said.

"Yeah."

"Then sure. Gloria's on night shift."

"I'm in," said Teresa. "Paul's got parent conference stuff tonight. Anything new come up for you today on the theater case?"

"Maybe," I said. "I'll fill you in."

We caravanned over there; since Sam lived in Glendale and Teresa lived in Tarzana, carpooling wasn't the most efficient idea. As usual there was a block-long queue for the drive-through, but plenty of parking in the lot. We went in, placed our orders, and snagged a table.

"How'd your thing go?" I asked.

"We're making progress. Pretty sure it was an inside job." Their other case was a jewelry-store burglary.

"None of the stolen stuff has turned up yet, though," said Teresa. "Makes it harder to pin it on anyone."

"Any employees refuse a property search?"

"No, they're all strangely cooperative," said Sam. We all laughed at that. Similar cases cropped up with some regularity; it was uncommon for stolen goods to stay with the thief more than a couple of hours.

"How about you?" said Teresa. "Anything popping?"

"I went through that schedule with a fine-toothed comb," I said. "And did a follow-up with Miz Salazar. Got some background on the financials and the casting. Two new names to look at there. But the key thing was confirming Hidalgo and Redding."

Teresa made a disparaging noise.

"You think she's got bad taste?" asked Sam.

"No, I think he's got bad taste."

Sam and I laughed. But I thought, having done those interviews myself, I understood where Marco's head was at. He was insecure, and probably a pushover for somebody like Redding. He wouldn't have questioned her motives. I said as much.

"Something ringing for you?" said Sam.

"Hey, until I was seventeen I was five feet tall," I said. "I know about wondering if anybody will ever say yes."

"At least you have a pretty face," said Teresa. "Unlike Mr. Bones here."

"Aw hey now, that ain't right," said Sam. "Just for that I won't ask you to Homecoming."

"Your wife would kill me if you did," said Teresa. "Come to think of it, so would mine. And don't tell Paul I said that."

We all laughed, but I had one of those moments. You know, the ones where you feel really lonely for a second. And yeah, I understood Marco.

V. Tanith

I got down to the theater at six-thirty, gave Mr. Cat a snack in the alley, checked on the dressing rooms, and did a walk-through backstage. Kevin came in about six forty-five and we had a brief confab. He was a friend of a friend, but not a personal friend of mine, which was what I needed in a stage manager for this project: someone who wouldn't spare my feelings or cut me any slack.

Fortunately, he hadn't found much to correct in my ideas for staging the piece. Or at least, if he had, he hadn't said anything.

Then I headed out to the house to take up my position. We had a tech box as close to the center as we could make it. This was made by reserving fourteen seats: six in our row, and four each in the rows immediately ahead and behind as a buffer zone. The box accommodated Brad's sound board, Valerie's controller, Yoshi's controller, and my Fortress of Obsession.

A thick bundle of cable snaked down the middle of the orchestra seating to the bottom edge of the stage, then up the sides to the house systems. Part of Kevin's job was to check the connections every time we came into the theater. Another part was to make sure the house switches got flipped at the right times. His copy of the script was so heavily annotated that it looked like a multicolored Rosetta stone. I'd taken a photo of that for the project page, too.

Yoshi, Brad, and Valerie all got there right before seven to set their stuff up. Kevin joined us just as

Lesley and Red skidded in. "Where were you guys?" I asked, half kidding.

Lesley said, "Red's car wouldn't start. I had just left, so he called me and I went back to get him."

I didn't like that; Red took good care of his car. But I couldn't whip out my phone and call the cavalry, and besides I would probably see the cavalry later. Which would explain why I again was wearing something colorful and flattering, instead of a tired old tee shirt. I told the others, "So the detective may be here tonight, in a sort of unofficial capacity. Don't pay him any mind, but if he asks you something please give him what he needs. Red, could you and Kevin go and make sure all your stuff is where it needs to be, and Lesley, could you just double-check the racks and make sure we have enough space for all the costume when it goes down tomorrow?"

The following night was our dress rehearsal. The action of the play took place on six different days, which meant six costumes each for the two leads. My villain, my ingénue, and my stripper each had four big scenes, so four changes each. The four showgirls had four group numbers – sixteen more costumes there, though the pieces were mostly pretty small. The lounge singer had three numbers; and the social dancers (five men, three women) needed four changes. Oh yeah, plus there were my two featured dancers, who had four changes.

It was a lot of costume, and much of it was provided by the actors or dancers. Everything needed to be tagged and bagged so that stuff didn't get mixed up. The last thing I needed was for somebody's corset or shoes, or the vintage Armani suit Lesley found for Ivory, to go home with somebody else.

Lesley and Red were both giving me The Look. I cringed. "I know, I'm sorry, I know." I was a micromanager. I couldn't help it, but I was usually better at not being obvious.

Having silently established their complete mastery of their domains, Red and Lesley headed off to the stage. Then Lesley turned around. "Am I doing makeup tomorrow too?" Asking me a question, throwing me a bone.

"No," I said. "Everybody's doing their own."

"Thank all the gods for that," she said, and continued on backstage.

The only people with serious makeup were the stripper, the lounge singer, the ingénue, and the showgirls. (For the showgirls it was really serious makeup.) But they all had a lot of experience doing their own, and we'd talked through what was needed during rehearsals. I made a note to stock up on cotton balls, tissues, and makeup remover.

I knew I didn't need to worry about putting together a wardrobe emergency kit. Lesley could assemble a reasonable facsimile of Marie Antoinette out of what was in her rolling bag.

As I finished the note I was aware that actors had been assembling. Kevin called everybody to the stage and I looked up to make sure everybody was there. It was a relief to see every face I expected. Plus Anthony, the social dancer who was helping out with props. And what do you know, there was Dexter.

Dexter, as Waiter 2 and a dance-hall customer, didn't have any lines and his business was pretty trivial. He was a fill-in for 'Larry,' one of my featured dancers, but Felipe (the guy who played Larry) wasn't called tonight, so I hadn't called Dexter in either. With Red to fill the Mickey/Waiter 1 parts I hadn't seen the need to call Dexter as understudy for the Henchman.

Every person who was called was a person I had to pay, so it wasn't a case of Aw how cute, he can't stay away. I wondered why he was there. Evidently, Kevin did too, because after everybody else dispersed they had a little confab. Dexter nodded at something Kevin said, and they both went off left.

I thumbed my walkie. "Kevin. What gives?"

"Dexter offered to help fill in and I kind of think we can use him tonight. People are a little scatter-brained. Is it okay or should I cut him loose?"

I thought for a second. We didn't really need him, but I needed drama less, and we could afford it. "The contingency will cover it. Let's keep him. Ready to go?"

"Give me five."

"Okay. Whenever you're ready."

We got underway at seven-thirty, which was pretty damn good all things considered. Theoretically tonight would go faster; we'd do each setup, confirm all the cues, and then move on without playing through all the dialogue or whatever. (Except of course for the few scenes with integrated cues. I'd simplified a lot from the first-final version of the script, because I couldn't afford two full days for tech. There is a lot of expedience in theater.) Just as the first song was starting, I heard footsteps in the aisle. I looked over and there was Sid. He sketched me a wave, indicated he'd take a seat nearby, and did so. I returned my attention to the stage.

Everything was running fine. Our collapsible phone booths were causing a little trouble (yeah, I know, phone booths – but cops didn't have cell phones in the Eighties). Since Dexter was there, Kevin used him to help Anthony and the set changes went fast.

The main set was: a performance area upstage; seating for social dancers downstage right; an open area at mid-stage; and a bar setup downstage left. The Million Dollar is a flat-front stage, which meant all the action happened basically inside a box. Our challenge had been to transform the box into a three-dimensional space where all the different moving pieces could be clearly seen.

Just as importantly, the box representing the dance hall had to be easily transformed from its early-evening, social style to the edgier after-hours. I had come up with what I thought was a pretty ingenious way to achieve that with lighting and a single set piece.

Thus my one big splurge was a neon sign centered above the performance space, which changed from 'The Blue Note' (in blue, of course) to 'The Black Box' (in red). Red had rigged a long power cord that was carefully fixed to non-moving parts of the backstage area, clipped and taped and flagged at its plug-in end with a big, black-on-orange DO NOT TOUCH.

The scenes that were not 'Blue Note' or 'Black Box' were minimal: an office space; a café; and a street.

So aside from the neon, our set pieces were: café tables and chairs, with a back flat; a rollaway bar with a backbar flat and some stools; some office furniture and a reversible flat; and an elevated stage platform, two steps high. The steps were separate pieces that locked into the sides of the platform, which could be tipped onto its back and then rolled off to the left wing. Red was really proud of it, and it helped a lot to give the Black Box Girls some stature.

It was supposed to be moved off (and then back on) at three points during the show. We hadn't moved it for first tech, but this time we needed to fit it into the process. If it didn't work – if it was too noisy or took too long - the plan was to drop a flat fabric panel called a scrim in front of it and just play all the non-dance-hall scenes in front of the scrim.

So anyway, the prologue scene was played in front of the scrim. Scene six, a short one on an office set, and scene ten (on a street) would be too, but that platform was supposed to move off after the Black Box Girls did their number in scene eleven. Something went wrong.

V. Ysidro

I had a feeling that crash, while the stage lights were off, was not part of the staging. Tanith sat up with a start, and I was out of my seat. We got to the stage at the same time and I caught her as she stumbled going up the stairs. "Careful there," I said. I set her back on her feet and she finished the climb.

"Thanks," she said over her shoulder, her attention all on Warner. Jackson had popped the stage lights back on almost immediately, and we could see that the platform had not rolled as I assumed it was meant to. It was out of position by about eight feet. Warner was cradling his right arm and looking pale, even for him. Parker and Anthony, the social dancer, were also standing by. I combed my brain for his last name because I knew I'd have to write this up. Roberts, I thought. Tanith had her hand on Warner's back and was saying, "What happened?"

"Wheel came out of its socket." He turned his head toward her. I couldn't read his expression aside from a clear 'that fucking hurt.'

Jackson nodded. "The whole thing tipped. He got out from under just in time."

Tanith asked, "Is your arm okay?"

"Just a scrape, I think. I'll have a hell of a bruise."

"You guys all right?" Now she was looking at Parker and Roberts. They both nodded.

Roberts said, "We each had an end and Red was in the middle. When it went all wobbly we weren't expecting it and couldn't hold the weight. Sorry."

"Not your fault," said Warner.

"Okay," said Tanith. I swear I could see her thinking. She turned to look out into the house. "Yoshi! You've got all the geometry figured out, right? To put the backgrounds on the scrim?"

He seemed to know what she meant because he called back, "Yeah, I'm good. I'll start programming the changes now."

"Thanks!" She turned back to the group onstage. "I don't want to be all 'the show must go on,' but can you put it back now? I mean, put it back in position. We'll just leave it in place like we did Monday, no moves, shallow stage for all the office and street stuff, fuck it."

"Yeah, we can get it." Warner moved toward the platform.

I cut him off. "Let me give you a hand with that."

Then he tried to go around to the back, and Jackson shouldered him out of the way. Warner laughed a little and stood back. Between the four of us (all smaller guys) we lifted it up, tiptoed it back out to the tape line on the stage, and carefully set it down. Then Warner locked the steps back into place. He was favoring his right arm, but his hand seemed to be working all right.

"Surface okay?" Jackson said, looking at it. The sides looked sound. All four of us climbed up on top and jumped up and down.

"Seems to be," I said. I noticed Warner picking something up off the floor under the back curtain. As we stepped down and I headed back out to the seats he followed me, handing over two heavy bolts.

"Those should have been in the caster," he said in a low voice.

"You'd have been flatter than Wile E. Coyote if Parker weren't here tonight," I said.

73

"Don't I know it." He went back up on stage. I turned to find my seat and Tanith was there.

"What did he give you?" She put a hand on my arm, looking worried.

"Someone took the bolts out of the middle caster."

"Dammit!" She lowered her voice. "His car wouldn't start tonight."

Worry was ratcheting up to anxiety. For some reason I didn't want to see her fall apart. "Take a breath." She did, letting go of me. "Run the show."

She scowled at me. "He's one of my best friends."

"He's okay. Run the show."

She sighed, thumbed her walkie, and told Jackson to proceed with the next scene.

The leads were a little rattled (of course, everyone there had come rushing up or out to see what had happened) but they carried on. Warner did his business one-handed as the waiter in the next-to-last scene. Interestingly, Parker seemed very composed as Waiter 2. I wondered if helping to save the day had been part of a plan, or if he was currently riding a wave of White Knight.

Then came the closing number of the first act, a ballad with a Latin arrangement that I liked. The leads sang the hell out of it. The main curtain came down, and the house lights came up.

"Fifteen minutes, everybody," Jackson called out before coming down to join Tanith. "You want anything, boss?"

"No, I'm good, thanks. See you in a few." He headed up the aisle. She talked briefly with the sound, music, and lighting people and then they went out too.

She slumped back in her seat and closed her eyes. I made a couple of notes and watched her for a minute.

"Want to take me backstage?" I said.

"Might not be a bad idea," she said. She pulled a bottle of water out of her bag and took a long drink, and then we went up onstage. It was hot from the stage lights. As we headed toward the makeup room I saw something move. "Okay, really," she said. "Mr. Cat, who keeps letting you in here?"

I made another note, mental this time; I needed to find out who'd gone out to the alley.

"And what is your name anyway," Tanith said. "I can't keep calling you Mr. Cat." She looked at the cat. He looked back up at her and said something. "Eiyrt?" she said. "That's your name?"

I couldn't help laughing. "That sounds like the farmer's wife in 'Men in Black.'"

"It does! What was his name really ... Edgar."

The cat chirped again; maybe he approved. I started toward the dressing room. This was entertaining, but I knew Tanith was stalling, and we didn't have much time. She fell in behind me and, when I looked back, so did Edgar. He didn't follow us downstairs, though.

Everything looked normal in the dressing rooms, I guess, because Tanith didn't say anything. She led me into a room that must have been under the left wing of the stage. It was low-ceilinged and dark, and none too clean. It smelled like dust and mildew, with a sweet undertone of spilled cola. Out the other side, there was a narrow flight of stairs up to the left wing. Washington had mentioned the space, but hadn't done it justice. "What's this space used for?"

"I think it's where you store your vampires," she said. "People only come through here if they have an entrance or exit from the left wing. You may have noticed there's not really room to pass behind the back curtain."

I had noticed that. You could pass, but it would be hard to do without being seen. Getting from an exit at stage right to an entrance at left would mean bolting down the dressing-room stairs, across the crypt, and back up the stairs on the other side.

"Did you set your entrances and exits taking that into account?"

"Yeah, I didn't want people going up and down the stairs any more than absolutely necessary. They're the worst thing about this place. Leftover from the days when actors were somewhere below blacks, Chinese, and Irish on the social-desirability scale."

We found the left wing cluttered with set furniture and props and littered with empty soda cans, chip bags, and coffee cups. This area smelled like paint and Fritos. "Does anything look out of place? Is this all from your people?"

Tanith shoved some litter out of the way with her foot. "Not really, believe it or not, and probably. Red did quite a bit of the set assembly here. He's great, but not always on top of the housekeeping. I asked him once, and he said he'd rather clean it all up at the end of the project than waste time on it every day."

Being a guy, that made perfect sense to me. "Okay if I hang around backstage and ask a few questions when people come back?"

"We need to know who went out the alley door, don't we."

I could have corrected her, saying *I* needed to know. I didn't. "We kind of do."

VI. Tanith

Act II went great. I was prepared for another disaster, but even the phone booths worked. Yoshi had tweaked the (remote-controlled; technology is awesome) projector rig so that the backdrops hit the scrim just right.

The theater's lights were pretty basic. I guessed that any production with special needs ended up bringing in their own stuff. We had several workarounds, suitable for a small budget, in place.

For the office scenes, a bar of harsh white lights at center stage was used. It delivered the unflattering fluorescent effect quite nicely, and left the rest of the stage in shadow. The projections for those scenes were of different nighttime-skyline views.

The club scenes were lit with a combination of the theater's lights and our own. Yoshi and Red had set up a few halogen pin lights for the showgirls' numbers on their platform, and the platform itself had a battery-powered rope light tacked to the front edge which was switched on for their numbers. We also ran out a sheet of silver-finished bead curtains behind the platform. Cheap molded plastic, but they read with a lot of sparkle in front of the back curtain.

The social dancers' tables had LED candles. The flat for the back bar also had some built-in LEDs, and there were more halogen pins above the rollaway bar.

For the scenes with the phone booths, we used two of the theater's bar lights – with yellow-white gels to look like streetlamps – just offset from the booths, so that the actors were in a sort of diagonal shadow; plus there was fill light provided by an LED kit built into each booth.

And finally, we lit the restaurant with a couple of strings of plaza lights and some re-staging of the LED candles, giving it a little fill from the theater's lights overhead. A projection of a block of mid-twentieth-century city buildings framed the café set.

Kevin and I had both been up to the catwalk before first tech to see where everything was. Yoshi was another OCD kind of guy and every fixture and cord was neatly marked. He had everything diagrammed on his laptop controller.

When we got to the end of the run-through, I really didn't have many notes to give. There'd been minor bobbles with the moveable set pieces, a sketchy line reading here and there, but the actual tech stuff was pretty much on point. And everyone had worked so hard that I took the time to tell them how good they were.

"I want to give a special thanks tonight to Anthony and Dexter. Anthony stepped in to help with the props, and Dexter came tonight because he was worried about us. And between them they kept Red from getting squashed like a bug, so thanks, guys." There was applause from everybody else. I looked around and realized Sid was nowhere to be seen. "Now does anybody have any questions for me? Anything on costume or makeup or marks or timing or whatever. We have some time yet tonight."

"I have a question," said Kevin.

"Yeah?"

"Why don't we have a trash can in the left wing?"

"That's a really good question. Probably the answer is because there are not supposed to be any refreshments taken to the left wing."

There was a chorus of Oops and Whoa and Sorry.

"I'll clean it up tonight but let's be conscious of that, please, people," said Kevin. "And I'll mention it to the others."

Then, "I have a question," said Anthony.

"What's that?"

"We're not supposed to go out the emergency exit, are we?"

"No, I'd much rather anyone who wants a smoke break use the side door in front of the backstage bathroom on this level."

He nodded but didn't say anything else. There were a couple more minor questions, then I dismissed everybody. I caught up with Anthony. "Why did you ask about the emergency exit?"

"Well, I saw that Susan girl going out after scene six. I didn't think she was even called tonight. I mean, she wasn't on in the 'In the Night' scene."

"She wasn't. Thanks for letting me know. And thanks again for your help tonight."

"No problem. I'm having fun," he said, smiling. He offered his hand and I shook it, then watched him go. I thought he was the most observant of the amateurs; he'd paid attention to the schedule, the call sheets, and a lot of other details. I would probably use him again. If I were ever to get crazy enough to do this again.

As the side street door closed behind Anthony, Kevin came down from the stage. "Everybody's out. I did a walk-through."

"Is the cat still inside?"

"No, was a cat in here?" Not really interested, he went over to the side door and gave it a solid tug, making sure the lock engaged. "Okay, I'm out. See you back here tomorrow."

"Thanks Kevin." I turned to collect my stuff, and saw Sid coming down the aisle. "Where have you been?"

"Up in the balcony area. Those bathrooms are pretty gothic."

I laughed. "Was it you who put Edgar outside?"

"Yeah, he wasn't too happy with me. I did another round backstage, went up to the second level. Not much to see up there."

"They spent a lot of money on the renovation, but really only to the point of being able to legally use and open the space. Nothing left over for frills."

"It reminds me of an old movie theater I used to go to when I was a kid."

"Did you grow up here in L.A.?" I wasn't sure why I asked. It was certainly none of my business.

He answered, though. "No, my family's in the Bay Area."

"My dad lives up there too. But I've always lived here."

"Your folks divorced?"

"Never married." We looked at each other for a minute. That little exchange, having so obviously nothing to do with the play or the theater or the investigation, was like opening a door. A door to what, I didn't know.

Sid's expression said he'd like to step through that door, wherever it went. "Want me to walk you out?"

"Sure." My car was parked in the lot right across the street from the theater. It was well-lit, for a parking lot, but still. It was late, and it was nice to have an escort. I specifically appreciated having this escort, and was sufficiently cognizant of the untimely nature of this appreciation that I told myself *down girl*.

"So how are you feeling about the show?" he asked.

"About the show, great. I'm pretty satisfied with how it's come together."

"I like the songs. You really wrote all those?"

"Yeah," I said, pleased.

"Of course, I also like the showgirls."

I snorted. "Everybody likes showgirls. That's probably my one nod to being commercial with this production."

"I noticed they are featured on the lobby cards."

"Well, of course. I want to assure people they are getting at least some guaranteed sexiness." Oops, I thought, didn't mean to use the word 'sex.' He was smiling just a little.

"So I have to ask. There's so much dancing in this thing. Do you dance?"

Another moment of appreciation, that he had to ask that. Why did he have to ask that? Did I really have to ask myself? "I know how to dance. But no, I don't really dance."

"Why not?"

"Because there is only so much time in the day, amigo." I was laughing a little, getting an idea where this might be going. Was this why I had so casually mentioned that I was single, back during the first interview?

"How long has it taken for you to put this together?"

"Two years, off and on. One hundred percent on for the last six months."

"Maybe when it's all over, you might go out dancing." We were standing beside my car. I looked up at him. He was really good-looking. "If you think you might have some time then," he said softly. His gaze dropped to my mouth, and I lost the plot for a second.

Then I shook myself a little, and unlocked the car. Opened the door and threw in my bag. Got into the driver's seat. Turned around and looked at him. "I might."

He smiled, closed the door after me, and watched while I drove away. Which I know because I looked back. And then I looked forward, thinking about how this was the wrong time to be flirting with someone, and the wrong someone to be flirting with, and there was a song about this situation but it did not address the fact that someone was dead.

Would Billy have minded? I thought not. I suspected he would have busted a gut laughing. Of all the theaters in all the world, that cop had to walk into mine.

Billy would have loved Sid. I realized with a start that they had a lot in common. That dry sense of humor. That quick wit. That mild exterior over a core of toughness.

Goddammit, I thought, and wiped away tears.

VI. Ysidro

Well, that was interesting. I had not come to the theater tonight with any intention of asking Tanith out, because I absolutely shouldn't, and yet it seemed I kind of had. And she had just kind of said that might be a thing that could happen. It made the drive back to the Valley seem a lot less of a hassle. Watch yourself, I thought.

I turned around from seeing her off, and spotted Dexter the White Knight. He was standing by what I assumed was his car, about fifty feet away. He stayed there as I walked over to him. "What's up?" I said.

"I just like to make sure she gets into her car safely."

"Carrying a little torch there?"

He looked down, then up, a little defiant. "We were dance partners for a while. It's a special connection."

"You know," I said, "there's a fine line sometimes between being a concerned friend and being a stalker."

Unsurprisingly, he was outraged. "I'm not a stalker!"

"Look, I've heard stuff in the past couple of days. It's obvious you care about her, and you were solid tonight. But I promise you, if she spotted you hanging around in the dark waiting for her, it would not make her feel safer." He looked away for a moment, then sighed. "The best thing you can do is be great in the show, and be a friend. Just a friend." It felt kind of mean, especially after my own conversation with Tanith, but it was the truth.

He knew it was. He nodded. "I know you're right." Maybe it was because he was an actor and a dancer, but his whole body seemed to express resignation. I wondered if I would have noticed, if this case wasn't about a play.

I patted him on the back. "Take it easy, buddy."

He got into his car, started it up, and drove off. I wondered if I would be able to take my own advice. Watching, and listening to, the rehearsal had been helpful in establishing who was where at any given time. But I couldn't swear that my mind had been a hundred percent where it should have been, which was on the investigation. If it had been, I wouldn't have been asking the director if she danced.

The next morning, I went into the station and met up with Washington and Muñoz. "What've you got for me?" I said, sitting down with my Starbucks coffee. (Don't judge. You wouldn't drink station-house coffee either.)

"Some more background on some of the players, and something interesting about that Susan Redding," said Sam.

"Oh yeah?"

"It seems she had a big part in a play back home, but only after the girl who originally got it had a freak accident and broke a leg."

"Freak accident, huh." We nodded wisely at each other.

Teresa said, "You guys seen that movie 'Showgirls'?"

"Of course," we said together.

She rolled her eyes, then asked "That what you think's playing out, Sid?"

"It seemed like the only obvious thing. Except neither of the men in line for the part Billy West was understudying really pinged me. The guys who weren't cast, I'm writing off – one got a job on a TV show that shoots in Vancouver, and the other one's doing a Beatles tribute show in Laughlin. And let me tell you what happened last night."

They took in the news about Warner's mysterious car trouble and the case of the falling platform. "But still, no ping on this Hidalgo?" Sam asked.

"I think he has an idea what's going on and is scared shitless about it. He seemed pretty rattled after the thing last night. But I don't think he's the instigator."

"Personally, this Redding has my antennae up," said Teresa. "She's not a nice girl."

"No, she isn't. And she and Hidalgo definitely have something going on."

"She could have gotten the oxycontin. She had access to West's drink. She's got her own car and lives in the Valley not far from Salazar and Company." Sam ticked off the points.

"I think we need to dig just a little deeper on her. If she's our perp, all we have is circumstantial. We need to establish a pattern, pin down a motive."

"Anything else?"

"I'd like a little more on Dexter Parker. He played the hero last night, but then I caught him hanging around the parking lot waiting for Salazar to leave. I think it's just puppy love, but I'd like to know if anyone's ever filed a harassment complaint or anything like that."

"I can call my contact at the union," Teresa suggested. "And Sam, don't you know somebody who knows somebody who works on American Idol?"

"Yeah. I'll reach out and see if anybody has any gossip about Miss Susan." He started to get his gear together, then stopped. "Oh, and Sid?"

"Yeah?"

"I talked to Mr. Song again. He corroborated what Garcia said about him and West planning to work together if they could. They had set up a dinner to talk about it next week, the three of them."

"Okay, thanks," I said. "I'll hit Garcia with it one more time, but it's not sounding like he was playing the homewrecker. And I'm going to advise him and Warner to watch their backs. Incidentally, guys, you should see this show. The hero is a singing, dancing cop."

They both laughed, and went to get started on their projects. I called Red Warner and recommended he keep some people around him. He said he wasn't going anywhere alone. I asked how his arm was doing, and he said, "It hurts, but it's working."

I said, "Glad to hear it," and got off the line. Then I called Victor Garcia and asked if he had a minute to meet, because the phone and the Internet are great investigative tools, but sometimes nothing beats a personal visit. He proposed we meet at Zankou Chicken in West L.A., which wasn't super convenient. But the alternative was doing this over the phone, and I wanted to see his face when we talked. I told him I could be there in half an hour, and he said that was fine.

He was there when I arrived. "What's up, Detective."

"I wanted to run something down for you. Sunday night someone, almost certainly a member of the cast, put oxycontin in Mr. West's chai tea latte."

"I heard that."

"The grapevine works fast, huh. We talked to Mr. Song about this project you and Mr. West had discussed."

"They were excited," he said, looking sad. "It would've been a cool project. Billy would have been, like, the Keyser Söze. The part I was looking at was the fixer."

"You're not still going to audition?"

"I ... haven't decided."

I nodded and moved on. "Monday night was this first tech rehearsal, and everyone found out about Mr. West by the next day. Tuesday Mr. West's fill-in, Red Warner, was officially assigned two parts in the show. Now Mr. West was also, and maybe primarily, an understudy for your part. Have I got that right?"

"Yeah. Billy and Tanith were family, and she hadn't seen anybody else who she wanted to double my part, so she asked him to do it. He was happy to."

"So there wasn't someone who auditioned for the Ivory part who isn't in the show at all, and might be out there holding a grudge?"

"Not as far as I know. It seemed like a pretty small group at the casting call. I know there were a lot of singers who couldn't act or dance. A lot of, well, kind of marginal people. The situation, you know."

"What do you mean?"

He ran down a list for me. "Set in the Eighties. Self-produced. A first-time director, with a show she wrote. A musical, and original songs. A lot of people probably saw that and thought it was just a vanity project."

"Is that what you'd say?"

"Hell, if I could write a show for myself I sure would. I've been in the business for seventeen years.

My agent said 'don't you dare,' but it's a good little part for me. And there aren't all that many world-premiere plays that come my way. So I'm cool." He smiled. "Since it started coming together I'd say I've been in much worse shows."

Yeah, I thought, this guy is not the problem. "I understand Mr. West's take on your part would have changed the, what would you call it, flavor of the show quite a bit."

"Yeah, it would have, but not to the point that anyone else would have to change the way they were playing their parts. If that makes sense."

It kind of did. "Okay. So then, there's this third person down the line, this Marco Hidalgo. He has a small part but he's doubling the two small roles that Billy West had. Now he's doubling them for Red Warner. As far as I can tell, the only reason for someone in the show to kill Mr. West was to move somebody into the parts he was playing. Also as far as I can tell, Mr. Warner could have had those parts from the get-go."

Garcia's eyes narrowed. "Yeah, he could. He and Tanith are tight, he could have had any part if he'd really wanted it."

"So it seems unlikely to me that Mr. Warner would poison Mr. West to get one step closer to your part. He told me he didn't want your part."

"He didn't. Red's a good actor, but the big impact in the Ivory part is from the songs. And Red, he can put across a certain kind of song, but these two songs are more in my wheelhouse. Lucky for me," he added.

"And it's highly unlikely that he would have seen missing a rehearsal, or getting injured in rehearsal, as a good way to move up to your part even if he wanted it."

"That would have been crazy."

I let the word dangle there for a second. I wanted him to think about what it took to poison and sabotage. Then I said, "Would you say that the road to success as an actor is knowing where your strengths lie?"

"I would."

"And would you say Mr. Warner is very clear on his strengths?"

"I would."

"So who in that cast is not so clear? Because if we take Mr. Warner out of the line of succession that leaves Mr. Hidalgo, and Mr. Hidalgo also told me that he didn't want the Ivory part. He said he's not ready for it."

"He's right."

Garcia was quiet for a moment, studying me. I'd seen on IMDB that he had a long list of crime drama roles, and I had an uncomfortable feeling I was going to be part of his current role. "Help me out here, Victor."

He sighed. "There's a certain type of person that you see sometimes. They maybe have a degree of talent, but they attach themselves to people who have more talent than they do. They may not even realize that's what they're doing. Sometimes that turns into this displaced ambition. They get excited about what the other person can achieve, and they can push people into doing things they wouldn't ordinarily do."

"Or maybe take matters into their own hands?"

He nodded slowly, meeting my eyes. "In theater, that's often your villain. Lady Macbeth. Iago. The motivation can be whatever, but the mechanism is the same."

Did not expect that, I thought, glad I knew enough about Shakespeare to get the references. "Miz Salazar told me she advised you to keep away from the rest of the cast."

"She did."

"I'd second that advice."

VII. Tanith

Dress rehearsal day. There was no new bad news in the email in-box or waiting in my text messages. Red's arm was completely black and blue, with a hideous swatch of raw red, but he said quite firmly that he was okay. Still, I felt so bad that I fixed him breakfast.

After that, he called AAA and they came out to check on his car. They found that the ignition wires had all been cut. This wasn't something they just carried around, so they had to tow him to the nearest full-service garage. "You might want to put your car under cover in future," the driver said. "This type of hood is too easy to pop."

Red looked sadly at his vintage El Camino, and got into the cab of the truck.

"You know," said Lesley when they were gone, "the problem with all this crap that's happening – I mean aside from the fact that it's crap – is that it's all really obvious and stupid."

"I know. There is no reason for anybody who's not in the show to try to interfere with the show, ergo whoever is interfering is in the show. It's a pretty limited pool."

"Do you know who's doing it?"

And right as she asked that, I remembered what Anthony had said about seeing Susan at the theater the night before. I'd forgotten all about it while I was talking to (okay, flirting with) Sid. "Sorry, Lesley, I have to make a phone call." I went to my room, closed the door, and dialed.

He answered right away. "Good morning, Miz Salazar."

"Good morning, Detective," I said, thinking he must have someone official in the room with him. "I forgot to tell you something last night. Anthony, the social dancer and new props guy, told me he saw Susan Redding leaving the theater by the emergency exit door last night."

"When?"

"About eight-fifteen, after scene six. That's an office scene. The scrim would have been down."

"Thank you, this is extremely helpful. How is Mr. Warner this morning?"

"He's Technicolor but functional. And his car was vandalized. He's at the garage with it now."

"Did he report the vandalism?"

"What, to the police? I don't think so. Oh, crap, he should have, huh?"

"I know ordinarily a police report on something like that would be a waste of time, but under the circumstances it's worth a shot."

"I'll have him call you with the garage info, maybe there's still time to take a look at it?"

"Okay. It's only fair to tell you, we have a suspect but we have no evidence. We are still investigating." He paused for a moment. "By the way."

"What?"

"Is there anybody in your cast who has not changed their name?"

I laughed. "Oh come on. There can't be that many."

"Miz Salazar, I was surprised to find that even *you* had changed your name."

"You have to admit it has more panache this way."

"Just so you know, in any other context, this would seem like very suspicious behavior." That smile was lurking in his voice. He must be alone now.

"Then it's a good thing this is show business," I said cheekily.

"With your permission, I'll come to the theater again tonight."

"You're welcome to."

"At seven again?"

"That's right."

"What are you doing the rest of the day?"

"I'm going over to see Uncle Kyong, as a matter of fact."

"Ah. Please tell him I hope to have a resolution for him before the end of the week."

"Thanks. I will." My call-waiting buzzed. "I'm sorry, I'm getting another call."

"Then I will see you tonight." He disconnected. I clicked over to the incoming call; it was Red.

"Everything okay?"

"Nothing else was messed with, if that's what you mean. They're going to replace the whole spark-plug-ignition assembly. Can you come and pick me up?"

"Sure. I'll be there in a few. Oh wait – which garage is it again?" He told me where to find him. "And Red, call Detective Palacio right now and let him know where you are. He wants someone to take a look at the car, maybe dust for fingerprints or something. Whatever."

He agreed, and I clicked off so he could get to it.

Forty minutes later, with Red disposed of, I headed to the other side of the 405, to where Billy had lived with Kyong. We'd talked on the phone but I hadn't seen him yet. I was appalled when he answered the door; he had aged twenty years.

He was hanging tough, though. I guess when your parents were refugees from a horrible war, you grew up as a constant target of discrimination, and your primary relationship had to be kept secret for most of your adult life, you got used to dealing with shit.

I told him how the show was going, and what Sid had said. "I really think he knows who did it," I said. "They just have to get enough to charge the person."

"Your friend Red, he's doing well?"

So then I had to tell him about the accident, if you could call it that, and the vandalism.

"Are you safe?" he said, looking worried.

"Oh my goodness, yes. If what is happening is what I think is happening, the bad guy isn't even paying attention to me. Besides, I'm surrounded by guys who are on high alert. Even my amateur dancers are playing cop."

"So your dress rehearsal is tonight."

"Yeah. We're only adding a few people, and no scenes. I don't know if I should hope for a disaster or for a smooth run."

"Well you know what they say – bad dress, good opening night."

"I have to tell you, that has never worked out for me," I said. "Usually bad means bad. So I guess I'm hoping everything goes smoothly."

"You still want me to come to the Sunday matinee?"

"Oh, definitely."

"I would have liked to see Billy on stage again," he said, looking sad. I hugged him.

"So ... do you think you'll stay in this house?"

"Oh yes. This was our home together, for so many years. And I wouldn't want to leave my garden."

He had a point there. It was a smallish midcentury house on a largeish corner lot, and Kyong had landscaped every inch of the lot. People routinely slowed down to look as they passed, and often stopped to talk to him if he was out in the yard.

"Well, you know I'm only a few minutes away. So if you ever want some company, give me a call."

"You are a sweet girl. I know you are busy. I'll see you on Sunday."

"Okay, Uncle." I hugged him again and went away before the tears got the best of me. If he could keep it together, so could I.

VII. Ysidro

We got lucky on the car. A tech guy got over to the garage, and among the prints left by Warner and the tow driver (who grudgingly gave a set for comparison) we found a third set.

The right thumbprint of that set happened to match a thumbprint on the lid of the coffee cup we'd found with Billy West.

Now all I needed to do was match it to one of the people in the show. When I briefed my commander, he cleared my overtime to attend the dress rehearsal. I checked out a crime-scene kit and enough supplies to fingerprint everybody, if I chose to. But I had an idea that I could get what I needed without letting anybody know what I was doing.

It was a good day otherwise, too. I got an official statement from Roberts on the Redding sighting. Sam pulled in some interesting gossip from his American Idol contact. Unfortunately nothing specific: it was all in that 'we can't really tell you because we might get sued if someone finds out we told you' gray area. But enough to get an idea that Redding had made several serious un-friends in her very brief Idol career. The words 'entitled' and 'delusional' may have slipped out.

Also, Teresa's union friend was able to – in my view – clear Dexter Parker. He had a golden reputation. He also had a day job at Barney Greengrass, and Teresa had verified that he'd been on shift the previous day. He would not have had time to get from Beverly Hills to Van Nuys and then downtown for rehearsal.

I decided to tug on one more line, and called the stage manager. "Mr. Jackson, it's my understanding your job is basically to see everything and be everywhere, is that right?"

He laughed. "Close enough."

"I need your snap judgement on who in the cast would lie to cover up for somebody else."

"Whoa." He was quiet for a minute. "I don't know that I can productively answer that. What I could say is, there are a couple of people who have really, um, bonded during the process. And maybe that's a different way of answering the question."

"I wouldn't be surprised."

"Okay then. You've probably noticed that cast and crew don't mingle a whole lot."

"Yeah, we got that."

"But between us, Red and Lesley and I are backstage nearly all the time. Lesley's probably told you that Marco and Susan hooked up."

"Not in those words, no."

"Well, I can verify. They've been playing hands-in-pants ever since the cast party."

"Anybody else?"

"A couple of the social dancers are married. Anthony and Marilyn. You probably had that already."

"Yeah, we did."

"And then there's Pixie and Trixie."

"Who?"

He laughed again. "Those are their character names. Two of the showgirls, Sherry Toyama and Tasha Jefferson. They're a couple."

"They did not mention that, but then, we probably didn't ask."

"Is that the kind of stuff you needed?"

"You never know. Thanks."

I looked back over the cast list. I'd be seeing only a few new people onstage tonight, and everyone had now been interviewed. Tanith had mentioned that the dress rehearsal would be filmed. I had a hunch that if there were to be any other 'accidents,' they would not be onstage; our killer-slash-saboteur wanted the show to go on. Just with different personnel.

I couldn't get my head around that. I tried to relate it to being excluded from an investigative team, which had happened to me a few times. Did I take it personally? Sure, yeah - the first time. But after you get a little experience you start to see that there are good reasons to build teams a certain way.

There is never just one person who can do a certain job. The ways in which individuals relate to each other are the real keys to the ultimate success of the team.

But this line of thought kind of reinforced the conclusion I'd already drawn. This series of crimes was opportunistic, impulsive, and immature. There was really only one person in the cast who fit that description, and who also had something resembling a motive.

What I still had to figure out was whether it truly was a case of a sole practitioner, or if someone else was facilitating things. I thought it was the former, but we had to eliminate the latter. Because it would not look good to make an arrest and then have something else go wrong.

VIII. Tanith

Call time was seven o'clock again, but I was meeting the rest of the tech team at the Million Dollar at six. Our videographer would be there at six-thirty to set up, so we needed to make sure all our stuff was loaded and locked, and tech traffic kept to a minimum.

I gave Lesley a hand packing her car with all the costume paraphernalia she was bringing in. She assured me she had sent reminders to each player who was providing their own stuff, with checklists. Then she shrugged and said, "Somebody will forget something. It's inevitable."

"Well, if push comes to shove most of the parts can be played in street clothes," I said. "But it's the clothes that really establish the time setting, so, ugh." I hated these factors that I could not control. There were too damn many of them.

"Asses will be kicked as necessary," she promised. "At least there's no chance Miranda and Lily will forget their costume."

We were both confident about that; our lounge singer and stripper were using this show for their casting reels, which I was totally okay with. It was actually a good thing for me: the more people who saw the show, even if it was just a piece of it here or there, the more likely someone would remember who wrote, directed, and produced it. I was fairly content with my day job, but I lived for the outside projects.

All the crew felt the same way. There's only so much a website can do to sell your work if you don't have clips. When you're an independent contractor, as every one of them was, being able to put up video clips that showed the work on stage was an incentive to take the job. Every cast member who asked was going to get a copy of the dress recording; all it really cost was a blank DVD. Permission to use clips was written into the crew contracts.

But I digress. We were heading downtown for dress rehearsal in a caravan. Red was riding with Lesley again, no doubt bitching about the lack of leg room in her car, and I was driving myself in. To get around the temptation to make phone calls on the way, I sent a bunch of texts before I got on the road. Then I double-checked my own list, did a visual on my bag, walked around my car to make sure it looked normal, and started in.

For a Thursday evening at rush hour, the traffic was ... absolute hell. I got to the theater with no time to spare, and no time even to check on Edgar.

First priority: dump my bag at the tech box. Second: extract makeup room supplies and take them backstage. Third: go downstairs to check dressing rooms. Lesley was already almost done loading the racks. Her color-coded tags were a thing of beauty.

Fourth: back upstairs to do a visual on the set pieces. Even though I knew Red or Kevin would have done it, I tested every chair and stool – the last thing we needed was for a leg to 'accidentally' fall off and dump an actor or dancer. The box of glassware for the bar setup all looked fine: no cracks or chips or suspicious powdery residues. The bottles of 'liquor' that Tony and Liz would use had been brought in by Red (impatiently brushing off my solicitous inquiry, gee sorry I asked) in a locked case.

Then I needed to get out of the way, and I could see Jim the videographer coming down the aisle with his rolling box of gear. So I joined Brad and Yoshi and Valerie out at the tech box.

The next half hour was me staying out of the way and trying not to butt in while Jim did his setup and testing. Kevin dropped first one and then the other scrim, Yoshi played with the projections, Jim fine-tuned his digital camera; then Valerie launched some music and they did a sound check.

Cast members started arriving at about a quarter to seven. Jenny and Tony were already in costume for their first scenes. Red went downstairs to get into his Mickey gear. (A six-three, 205-pound guy makes a very believable cop. He had to wear a wig, though; the ponytail would interfere with the suspension of disbelief. Lesley had found a truly epic mullet.)

Lesley hit me on the walkie. "Jenny and Tony have all costume." I didn't respond; that was just an FYI.

Next in were Sherry and Tasha. I could see for myself they had all their costume. Not far behind them were Rita and Maria, the other showgirls. Rita stopped by me as they came down the aisle. "My Alley Cat corset has a tear, but I brought it anyway," she said. "It's not in an R-rated place."

"Lesley has her box of wonders. Let her know if you want it fixed."

She nodded and went on. I was marking off on my list who had arrived. There were a lot of ways out of the theater, but only one way in – the main lobby entrance. This had several advantages from my point of view, chief among them being that I did not need to be anywhere other than where I was supposed to be – in the tech box – in order to do a head count.

Dexter and Felipe and Cameron and Victor. All present and accounted for. Here was Miranda, hustling a little because she had a song in the first Blue Note scene and needed to get into costume. Her hair and makeup were already done, I noted. Lily was right behind her. She had on a kimono kind of deal and I assumed she was already in costume. She proved me right and cracked me up by going straight to center stage, dropping her bags, and flashing the house. Brad and Yoshi applauded.

The social dancers arrived in three groups: the two single women, the four single guys, and the couple. They were all carrying the bits and pieces they needed to make one or two outfits look like four. The prompt/runner gal showed up solo, looking like a ninja in low silent-soled shoes, black jeans, and a long-sleeved black tee.

"Those shoes are perfect," I called to her as she passed. She smiled and gave me a thumbs-up. I made another note. Betty had been a complete trouper after getting over the disappointment of not dancing. Someone who didn't need to be told things twice was always an asset.

Marco and Susan came in together. I made another note. Marco's character, the Henchman, always wore the same thing: a cheap black suit. But just in case, for Mickey and Waiter 1, he'd needed additional costume, and he was just enough bigger than Red that they couldn't share. For the Waiter all it took was to lose the suit jacket and add an apron. For Mickey, Lesley had located a glen plaid jacket and hat.

Susan's one scene was played in a club-style dress; you know, the kind of thing girls wear out when they're trying to pick up a guy or otherwise get attention. Apparently she had a lot of these because she never wore the same thing twice. Tonight's version was truly tramptastic; I had to hand it to her, it was perfect for the part.

She teetered down the aisle on stiletto-heeled platform pumps, and I thought, Idiot. And also, ew; they were beige patent leather. Not 100% period accurate: only an actual hooker would have worn those in the Eighties. It wasn't worth calling her up. I made yet another note, though: she couldn't wear those around backstage.

Liz – my other featured dancer - was the last to arrive, grimacing an apology. She was hauling ass, and gear, backstage. I thumbed the walkie. "Hey Lesley, how are we doing? Liz just got here."

"We are amazingly complete down here. Miranda is dressed. Give me five minutes with Liz and then you can call it."

"Okay. Oh hey."

"What?"

"Does Susan have some flats to wear backstage?"

"Yeah."

"Thanks."

I clicked off and sat there, thinking, wondering if I had forgotten anything. I'd been over the material so many times, and thought through all the logistics so many times, that I couldn't remember what I had done or when I had done it. I just had to trust that we were as ready as we seemed to be.

VIII. Ysidro

Tanith hadn't seen me come in, right behind Mr. Garcia. I was sitting in the back row of the theater and pretty much everyone had failed to notice me thus far. I thought that was probably good. But I did need to get my hands – and my kit – on a few things.

A few minutes after seven Tanith thumbed her walkie and spoke to someone. A few minutes after that, Jackson called all cast members to the stage.

It was surprising how they filled it out. And I had to repress a laugh at the costume – everyone, it seemed, had been able to create something that screamed '1980s' even when they weren't dressed by Ms. Hayes. The lead actress was wearing a big-shouldered red skirt suit, and big hair to match. The lead actor got off relatively easy in a blue Izod shirt, pleated pants and Adidas with a black Members Only jacket slung over his shoulder.

Tanith went up to the stage. Everybody made space.

"Hi everybody. Thanks for all your hard work. Tonight we're going to try to play it straight through, so if you flub a line or sing the same lyric twice, just keep going. As you know, we have a videographer here to record this for posterity."

There was a general groan, and some laughter.

"For those of you who haven't been here since Sunday," she went on, "you'll be noticing background music for the first time. We have instrumental tracks playing in scenes 2, 4, 8, 15, 17, 23, and 24. Social dancers, you are encouraged to act like you normally would when you go out dancing. Just remember that there will be dialogue in these scenes. Our audience needs to be focused on the people who are speaking, or on the business of the lead actors. Dancers, remember you are background."

They all nodded solemnly.

"We have installed buzzers on the seats of the café chairs and if Betty hears you talking she will be giving you a light shock." Sounds of confusion. "Not really." Laughter. "At least not tonight." More laughter. This woman knew how to work a crowd. "Any questions before we get started?"

Nobody seemed to have any.

"Okay then. Dress rehearsal, 'What Went Down.' Places please for prologue, and wings for Scene 1."

There was a scurry and hubbub as people sorted themselves out. This was when I needed to get backstage. Before Jackson got the main curtain down, I had mingled with the male dancers. They were all on in Scenes 1 through 4. Once they were in position onstage, I thought, I'd do a fade to the dressing room.

I was glad they were taping tonight, though. I'd gotten kind of invested in the show and hated to miss seeing any of it.

I knew Tanith would be back in the tech box by now. Jackson was standing in the right wing operating the curtain. When everyone was in position he spoke quietly into the walkie, and intro music started. I recognized the theme; it was from the lead actor's solo, called 'Suspicion.' After maybe two minutes, it faded, and the curtain opened.

The scene changes were done on blackouts, not by closing the curtain. The first blackout was when all the dancers took the stage. I hung back, sidled down the hallway above the dressing room, and waited.

Patience, grasshopper, I thought.

First song. Dialogue. Showgirls. Up came Ivory, Henchman, and Girl. Nobody looked to the left as they came up. I went down the stairs.

Susan Redding's dressing station was clearly marked. I couldn't believe my luck: under the counter was a pair of heinously ugly patent-leather stripper shoes. I hit them with the kit: took digital photos, then dusted, more photos ... and peeled off a gorgeous, almost-complete set of prints. Then I carefully put away the results and cleaned the shoes again.

I could hear Ivory (Garcia) singing upstairs. Damn, that guy had a great voice. He sounded like a cross between Nat King Cole and Marvin Gaye.

Someone was coming down the stairs. I planted myself in the middle of the women's area, trying to look like I belonged there. Hayes came through the men's area and did a double take. "Oh hey," she said. "Tanith didn't mention you'd be here."

"There was something I needed to check out. Can you verify something for me?"

"I'll try."

"These shoes." I walked over to Redding's station, beckoning Hayes to follow me. "Those are Miss Redding's?"

"Yeah. She wore them tonight but I put her in something else for her scene. She's a little pissed at me." Hayes didn't look too concerned about that.

We could hear feet moving in the right wing. The song was over. "I'm going up on the left," I said. "I'd appreciate it if you didn't mention I was down here."

"You got it." She nodded and I hustled out.

I wouldn't say I had memorized the scene order, but I knew that Redding was basically done for the night. There were several places she could spend the rest of the time. I wanted to try to keep an eye on her, without her being aware of it. I lurked in the crypt and watched as she came into the dressing room. She kicked off the shoes Hayes had given her, and slid into a pair of flats. Then she dug a pack of cigarettes out of her bag.

I didn't see what else she took out, but she was carrying something in each hand when she left the room.

I decided to go up to the left wing and watch the rest of Act I. Nobody else was coming or going from that side. If I remembered correctly, the ballroom dancers would all be on stage for the next few scenes and would go off right. I thought I was clear. But when I got up there I found the showgirls making adjustments to their costume.

It's not such a bad thing getting manhandled by four sexy women. They stuffed me into a corner, basically, and made me turn my back. I was trying not to laugh.

Fox (Cameron Monaghan) was finishing her first song. Then there was some more dialogue, and then the lead guy had his solo. Then a street scene. And then the showgirls went on for their second number. The lady dancers had left the stage, but the men were all on, acting like a pack of dogs. Parker was in there too.

After that came an encounter between the two leads, and then their song closing the first act.

Jackson dropped the curtain. I heard Tanith from the house call "Intermission. Notes, then break."

IX. Tanith

Act I went as well as I could have hoped. Nobody forgot a key line, all the songs were fine, there were no problems with the props. The music cues were all on time, the effects and balance were solid, the projections and lighting looked good. The only thing that gave me any anxiety was the fact that I knew I had a killer in my cast.

Really, just that one little thing.

I gave the cast some notes on the first act. Basically at this point, I thought trying to change anything would just create confusion. But there were a few mistakes to call out, and a few good things I wanted to reinforce.

"Phil, I like how you're macking on Liz. Keep doing that. Marilyn, keep playing hard to get with Anthony."

The dancers laughed.

"Marco, you're looming really well. Remember you're Ivory's one real ally here, you're not a good guy. You have a tendency to look sorry for Susan, don't do that."

"Yes ma'am."

"Miranda and Lily, you're both on point. Showgirls, everything cool with the platform?"

"It's fine," Rita said.

"Tony and Jenny, I love what you're doing. Victor, perfect as usual. Cameron, maybe dial back the weird just a tiny bit in your first scene so that the desperation makes more of an impression in the next one."

"Got it."

"Okay. Generally, everybody, you're awesome. See you back in a half hour."

Kevin led a round of applause for the cast and crew, and then everybody dispersed. I walked around the stage again, nodded at the arrangements the showgirls had made for an informal changing room in the left wing, snickered at the pile of dance shoes in the holding pen between the right wing and the makeup room. Then I pushed open the emergency exit door to see if Edgar was there. He trotted right in. "Hey buddy. Ready for your snack?"

We went into the makeup room, strewn with kit bags and amazingly littered (honestly, people, there's a wastebasket right there). I fixed Edgar his dinner. He made a point of thumping me on the leg before settling down to eat. I drank a bottle of water and tried not to think.

I was watching Edgar wash his face when there was a tap on the door. I looked up. "Hey, Sid." It was good to see him.

He looked like he was glad to see me, too. "Hey, Tanith."

"Everything okay?"

"As far as I've heard."

"Got anything new?"

"Not for sure. I have something to check out tomorrow."

"Great." We looked at each other for a minute.

"How's old Edgar, here?" he asked, coming into the room a few feet and bending to pet the cat. Edgar obligingly thumped him with his multicolored head.

"I'm totally taking this cat home at the end of the run."

Sid laughed, then sobered, looking at me with a curious intensity.

"What's up?"

"I'm having trouble keeping it professional, Tanith. I'd better get out of here for now. I'll check in after the show, okay?"

"Okay."

I stayed there, thinking happily distracted thoughts, till I heard people coming back. Then I escorted Edgar back to the alley. He sat down and stared at me with what looked a lot like reproach as I shut the door.

"Hey, Tanith?"

I turned around. It was Victor. "Yeah, what's up?" He seemed really mad.

"I found this in my bag downstairs." He handed me something. I looked at it. It was Lesley's bottle of oxycontin.

"Really?" I wasn't asking for verification from Victor, of course. I was asking the universe how anybody could be so effing stupid that they thought they could implicate Victor with this clumsy, obvious plant. I think he got that, because he kind of laughed. "Don't worry about it," I told him. "I'll tell Detective Palacio where it turned up."

"You know I would never have done anything to hurt Billy, right?"

"Of course. It's okay, Victor."

He went away, and I looked at the tiny pink pills. They looked almost like children's aspirin. So innocent. It was all I could do not to drop the bottle on the floor and stomp it to smithereens. Instead I looked for a paper bag to put it in. Didn't find one, of course; there was plastic everywhere, but no paper.

Until I got out to the tech box and found, on my seat, an El Pollo Loco bag with a note scrawled on it: EAT ME. I snorted. It had to be from Red. I pulled out the avocado poblano burrito and took a big bite, then made sure the inside of the bag was clean and dropped the pill bottle into it. I rolled the top loosely and stuffed the bag into the side of my satchel.

Either that was a really good burrito, or I forgot to have lunch. When I looked up from inhaling the burrito, Kevin had the whole cast assembled on the stage. He was talking to them. I gave him my prearranged signal – two quick taps on the walkie.

"Okay, people, beginners for Act II. Places please," he said.

Cameron basically opened the act, with her second song. The play didn't spell it out, but I hoped it was obvious her songs were supposed to be written by her character Fox. The first two were real emo ballads full of loss and longing and adolescent angst. You know how it is with your first big love – everything seems like the end of the world. Cameron really put it across.

Watching it through like this, I was reassured that the script was well balanced in terms of the music. There were seven musical numbers in each act. But in terms of the staging I'd overcomplicated things a bit in Act I by having a Black Box scene sandwiched by two non-club scenes.

Jeesch! I'm telling you, having a brain that won't shut off is not an unalloyed good.

But it was clicking along and everything was going fine. Then there was something a little funky between Felipe and Marco in Scene 17. What the hell? Felipe did his exit but with an irritated backward look. I'd have to find out what was up.

Good work from the showgirls. Ivory's killer (if I did say so myself) second song. Café, street scene, office. More bonding between the leads.

Cameron's final song, deep into the weird. This was a time when the dancers onstage were explicitly instructed not to dance: I had an action freeze, basically. I wanted the audience to get the sense that bad things really might happen. Valerie's arrangement was minimal, minor, and creepy. It was all I could do not to applaud.

The showdown between Evan and Ivory. A little brief, maybe not so satisfying, could be fleshed out. I pulled myself up short with a mental *stop it*!

Final number from the showgirls, completing their evolution from cute to trampy to vicious to tragic. Wrap-up at the café; where was Red? Dexter came on as the waiter. I started to panic.

And the closing ballad, happily ever after. Whew. Now, up onto the stage to find out what the hell happened to Red. I pushed through the dropped curtain to find him laughing his ass off with Anthony. He saw me coming and tried to look apologetic.

"I'm sorry, Tanith, I totally missed my cue. Anthony and I were moving the furniture and then I just went off with him. Fortunately Dexter was paying attention, he'd just come off from 'Alley Cat' and when he saw I wasn't in place he grabbed the apron and went on."

"Thanks, Dexter. That's twice this week you've pulled Red out of the fire." He nodded and made a gesture like 'no problem.' I gave a few notes, congratulated everybody again, and told them I had an idea.

"We still have an hour on the clock tonight. I don't want to wear you all out, but on the other hand there's something I think would work for the show that would actually make your jobs easier. I'm proposing to switch the order of scenes ten and eleven."

Kevin looked at his clipboard. "Putting 'I'm the One' right after 'Suspicion'?"

"Yeah. So we'd then drop the scrim and play through the street scene, Maestro's, and Act I finale with maybe a little more logic."

I let him think about it for a minute. He glanced at his watch, then looked up at the cast. "Everybody, I think this would be good. No need to change costume, but can we go back to the end of scene nine after Tony's song, do a quick transition with the lady dancers exiting, go straight into 'I'm the One,' then drop the scrim and carry on with the first street scene."

I nodded. "Let's see how it works. Showgirls, just mark it through."

So we did that; and it worked better. Valerie did an on-the-fly music cue using a snippet she already had edited. The social dancers improvised like champs. Yoshi did some magic with the lights, and presto change-o. I'd settled in the first row to watch, and scooted up to the stage as soon as the bits with the phone booths were done.

"Terrific, thanks everybody. Let's go with that for tomorrow. Everybody, mark up your scripts, like right now. I'll send an email to remind you, and Kevin will make sure the prompt sheets are updated. Right, Kevin?"

"Right."

We did the transition one more time, to give the dancers a chance to lock down their business; then I told everybody to go change. If it wasn't ready to go now, it was not going to be ready the following night. As people came back up in their street clothes, I dismissed them – all except Felipe and Marco. I made small talk with Felipe till Marco came up. "Okay guys. What the hell."

Felipe said, "Oh, you caught that, huh?"

"Yes, I caught that."

Felipe looked at Marco. Marco looked at the floor.

"Marco?"

"It was my fault, ma'am. I was crowding Mr. Matamoros."

"Why?"

"I was just a little distracted and didn't realize I was out of position."

"You can't be distracted, Marco. Not on stage. There are no take twos."

"I know, ma'am. I'm sorry."

"Don't be sorry, just be in it. Okay, guys. Take a hike. Get a good night's sleep."

"No way," said Felipe. "I'm going to a milonga."

I laughed, as he probably intended, and then Jim the videographer was coming up and I had a whole 'nother thing to talk about.

"Well, how's it look?"

"The projections came across super well," said Jim. "I know a dance company that's going to want to try that."

"Lighting okay? Does the sign show up?"

"The sign's great. I'll boost the light level and the contrast when I process it."

"How about the sound?"

"The feed Brad set up for me worked perfect. I wouldn't call it studio-quality, but I think you'll be happy with it."

"Okay. I'll look forward to seeing it. When do you think the four dance numbers might be ready?"

"If you don't want them processed, I can extract them and send you mp4s by tomorrow afternoon."

"Really? That would be awesome. Yes please." I stuck out my hand, and Jim shook it.

"This was fun. But I'm still gonna send you a bill."

"Yeah, yeah," I said, and he laughed as he left.

IX. Ysidro

I spent Act II picking up a few little trophies and otherwise stalking Redding around the theater. This was much less interesting than it sounds; she mostly sat in the makeup room or the holding area, with a side trip upstairs to the 'star' dressing rooms, which weren't in use for this show. I went back out to the house after Jackson dropped the curtain.

I listened to the notes, watched the proposed revision with interest. Then I eavesdropped on Tanith's come-to-Jesus with Matamoros and Hidalgo, and wondered why Hidalgo was distracted.

It occurred to me he had probably spoken to Redding during the intermission. Maybe I should poke him a little. I walked out to the lobby to see if I could catch up with him, and then started running when I heard a squeal of brakes, car horns, and women screaming.

At the corner of the street was a cluster of people, with Jenny Wilson at the center. I looked in every direction but didn't see anybody apparently hurt, so focused on the group. Matamoros, both Parkers, and Lily Chen were all there.

"Everybody okay?" I asked. They all looked over at me with surprise. I didn't see any reason to explain myself.

"Jenny had a close call," Matamoros said. "A bunch of us were waiting for the light to change, but right before it did she went flying."

"Someone pushed me," Wilson said. She looked shaken, edging toward angry. I didn't blame her.

116

"Did you see anybody?"

"No, I was too busy peeling myself off the hood of a taxi."

There was an amazing amount of foot traffic. It would have been surprisingly easy for someone to disappear if they timed it right. I looked down Third Street, then down Broadway; there were just too many people out and about. Sometimes I missed the old Downtown, empty after seven p.m.

"Tomorrow's opening night, right?" I asked. There was a chorus of yeses. Tomorrow was also Friday. I was on duty, and I knew I had to talk to a bunch of people all over again.

"If any of you remember seeing anyone or anything suspicious, give me a call tomorrow, okay?" I made sure they all had my number, watched the group go across the street and up to the parking lot, and then turned to go back into the theater.

Tanith was just coming out. "I hope you didn't leave anything inside," she said.

"No, I'm good. I was hoping to talk to you." I had my crime-scene kit and various trophies with me, in a backpack kind of deal.

She looked around. No other theater people were in sight. "Do you have anything new?"

"I won't be sure till tomorrow," I said. "And you should know there's a whole new round of interviews to do. Someone tried to push Miz Wilson under a taxi."

"What the fuck," she said wearily. "Enough already! I wanted to give you this." She handed me a crumpled El Pollo Loco bag. I looked at her questioningly. "Victor found the oxycontin in his bag when he came back from break." I looked inside the bag and sighed. "Yeah," she agreed. "He was pretty pissed off about it. But it's an obvious plant, right?" I did this noncommittal gesture and she gave me a dissatisfied look, then said, "I don't know if you can find any fingerprints, or whatever, but please get this out of my sight."

"Be happy to. Walk you to your car?"

"Sure."

So we walked. People had cleared out fast. The parking lot was nearly empty when we got there.

Tanith slung her bag into her car and then leaned against the side, holding the door open. "Did you see anything tonight that I need to worry about?" she asked.

"I think you're doing enough worrying for three or four people."

"I can't help it. It was one thing when I thought just Red and Victor might have to be on the lookout. Now Jenny too? How in the hell does – how would anyone think that taking Jenny out would get them anywhere?"

"Crazy and stupid go hand in hand an awful lot of the time, you know," I said. She laughed, like I'd hoped. "So when did you get the idea to switch those two scenes?"

"It jumped out at me after seeing the act played all the way through. It was clunky. All the dancers left the stage, and then we had to bring most of them back on one scene later, and the whole do-si-do with the scrim. Frankly," she said, looking animated, "Kevin should have called me on it. It's a rookie mistake."

"He probably thought it wasn't serious enough to get into."

"Yeah, whatever." She hmphed a little, and I laughed. "So listen. If you want to come tomorrow night I'll have a ticket held for you."

"I'll be here." We looked at each other for a long moment. I wanted to keep the conversation going.

Apparently she did too. "Okay, now I'm having trouble keeping it professional. So good night." She got into the car and closed the door. I watched her drive away.

And then I took my bag of death and headed back to the station. You don't fuck with the chain of evidence: it had to go straight in to be logged, and the forensics people would have it first thing in the morning. The desk guy stared at my stuff and then gave me a look.

"What?"

"Why you got six sets of prints here?"

"Elimination. Be pretty stupid to assume I know who I'm looking for, now wouldn't it."

He snorted. "Don't you wish it was like in the movies? You know who done it, all you got to do is haul them in?"

We agreed that real-life police work was sadly hampered by the need to provide enough evidence for a prosecutor to bring charges. I watched as he wrote up the log, put each piece in its appropriate carrier, and dropped them into the delivery cart. Then I said good night and went home.

I was feeling kind of wired. I was used to odd hours, but this investigation was not usual, with most of whatever mystery there might be solved by the physical evidence at the crime scene. I mean, you would be amazed at how sloppy most killers are.

And when you consider how most killings happen, it makes sense. There are very few criminal masterminds out there. Most people who kill do it on impulse. It's an emotion-driven, illogical, unplanned fit of I-don't-know-what-else-to-do. Even the gang-style shooting, my personal least favorite after a domestic, can be pretty easy to solve. Because let's face it, these guys tend to get in trouble over and over again, so we know them. We know where to apply pressure. In this case, we didn't have any leverage.

The one thing our suspect had done that was smart was use the full-cast read-through to poison the chai tea. That was the only thing that had happened so far that could have been done by just about anybody. And that was why we needed to establish opportunity for the other crimes, because we couldn't prove that Suspect A was the only person who could have done the main one.

I hoped Washington would come in tomorrow with another nail for the box. I'd asked him to take a uniform and canvass the Salazar neighborhood, try to find a witness to the vandalism of Warner's car. I'd called in a favor from the Downtown division too, doing interviews around the intersection where Jenny Wilson had almost taken her swan dive.

And I'd asked Downtown to also nose around about the evening of second tech, when Warner almost got flattened. We had an inside witness to our suspect leaving the theater, but a corroborating statement from outside would be helpful.

There's this assumption that modern life is self-involved, everybody on their cell phone, paying no attention. But somebody always sees something.

I kept going over it in my head, trying to think if there was some other thread to pull, but I wasn't seeing it. So I swung my kettlebells for a while, until my phone rang.

X. Tanith

I was utterly exhausted and yet not at all sleepy. Updated all my notes, sent out a dozen emails, picked out my clothes for opening night. Stretched for a while and decided to sign up for a dance class after the show wrapped. Didn't want to take Zzz-Quil again. What I wanted, frankly, was a good bounce.

That wasn't going to happen. The whole friends-with-benefits thing is a minefield; it wouldn't have been fair to Red, especially since I had someone else, someone specific, in mind. So I checked to make sure Lesley was done with the bathroom, found she was already in bed, and filled up the tub for a soak, et cetera.

Lying there, I thought back over the whole course of the production. I was pretty certain I knew who our bad guy was, and positive that Sid also knew, and oh how I hoped that I wouldn't have to face that when I got to the theater tomorrow night. What was I supposed to do if I did? If I got there and Susan was there, was I supposed to act normal, oblivious, clueless?

Not that I was normally oblivious or clueless. But this seemed like something I maybe shouldn't one hundred percent improvise.

Because I am unable to leave my phone for more than five minutes without having abandonment issues, I glanced at it lying on the toilet seat. Would Sid still be working? Would he talk to me? Should I call him?

My God, I thought; I was practically singing the Act I finale in my head. The hell with it. I dried my hands, picked up the phone, and dialed. He picked up after two rings. "You all right, Tanith?"

Wasn't that a nice way to answer? Oh how I wanted to say 'no I need you." Instead I said, "I need some advice. I'm sorry to call so late."

"No worries, I just got back from the station a few minutes ago."

"If ... everybody ... shows up tomorrow night, how should I behave? Business as usual?"

"That would be good."

"Should I be prepared to cover ... anybody?"

"Might not be a bad idea. I really can't say any more, though."

"Yeah, I get it. I'm just, well, you might have noticed I'm a planner."

"I did notice that." The smile in his voice; it got me every time. And did nothing to settle me down.

"Okay. I'm gonna let you go now."

"See you tomorrow."

"Bye." I clicked off, looked at the picture I'd taken of him that he didn't (I was pretty sure) know about, then shut down the phone.

I hadn't set my alarm but woke up at my usual time anyway. Body memory is both a blessing and a curse. Plus I was excited, in spite of everything. It was opening night day!

After a quick breakfast, I drove down to the Sepulveda Reservoir and took a long walk with my camera. It was still early enough to be decently cool, and not many people were out since it was Friday. Much nicer than on the weekend. I stayed out longer than usual.

When I got back, I needed a shower, and then I was hungry again. Red was finishing his breakfast. I sat down across from him instead of going through to the kitchen. "So is your car going to be ready today?"

"Should be. They're gonna call me. Will you be around?"

"Should be. How are you feeling about tonight?"

He shrugged. "I'm good. As long as nothing else happens."

"Ugh, I know." I knocked on the wood table.

"The scene swap last night was a good idea."

"Kevin should have called that out," I complained.

Red laughed. "You may not realize this," he said, "but you can be a little intimidating."

"What, me? That's ridiculous."

"Oh stop it. You've been working in the industry for thirty years, you've got a master's degree in theater, you've written and produced and directed this show. You really think a stage manager with half your experience is going to say oh hey, you know these two scenes should switch places, right?"

I was stumped for a second. "Well, when you put it like that."

He laughed again, and then I started laughing, and because we were both a little punchy we were both still laughing when Lesley came shuffling in. I gave her the once-over. "You were in bed before me, what's the zombie act?"

"I had the nastiest nightmare, you guys," she said. "I woke up at three in the morning, feeling like there was a monster sitting on my chest, and for a second I could almost see it."

"What did you dream?" I asked. "Unless it was about the show. Don't tell me if it was about the show."

"It wasn't specifically about the show, but I know it was about the show."

"Then let me grab my breakfast and get out of here so you can tell Red."

"I don't want to hear it," he protested.

"She needs to tell someone, Red," I said. "You know how the brain works."

"I know how your brain works, but I fail to see how that would apply to normal people."

I smacked him lightly (on his good arm) and went to assemble my food. Then I went back to my room, because I really did not want to hear about Lesley's nightmare.

Instead I got on the computer and started harassing my box-office and concessions team. I had taken a leap of faith and delegated everything (though with explicit instructions), but now the day was at hand, and I needed to know what I was going to see when I got to the theater.

Anyway, it was a relief and a pleasure to get back a detailed inventory, with images attached. The concessions person had asked if we had a tee shirt; I'd said no but they could get one if they wanted. They'd gone with a white and dark-red design printed on a black shirt. I liked it; it looked like an old detective comic, which in a way suited the material very well.

They had also done the postcards, lobby cards, and programs. Plus they'd have snacks and beverages. This particular outfit had a license to sell wine and beer, for which I was deeply thankful.

I sent back a blanket approval and note of appreciation, with a request to hold back tee shirts for the cast and crew. The reply came by eleven: *Already done.* Gee, I like working with people who think like me.

With that out of the way, I thought about how to cover the Girl if our Girl didn't show tonight. I didn't want to assume she wouldn't be there. I also didn't want to get caught flat-footed if she wasn't.

The problem was that every other featured female in the cast was really noticeable in her part. Jenny was the star, Liz was in thirteen scenes with dialogue and featured dancing, the showgirls were actually on in the Girl's scene, and Lily was unmistakable - quite apart from being on in seven scenes, including the four immediately preceding the Girl's scene.

That left Valerie, and she was a musician, not an actress. It seemed like the simplest thing was for me to play it myself. I could still pass for early twenties, especially with stage makeup. All I needed was a dress that said I Want to Be a Star and I'll Go with Sketchy Men if That's What it Takes.

But I did not own such a thing. And I couldn't ask Lesley to whip one up, because Lesley has many sterling qualities but discretion is not necessarily first among them.

So I threw myself together, breezed through the house with a "have to run an errand, be back soon!" and went shopping.

It had been so long since I'd been to the mall that I had to study the directory, and even then it took several attempts to find the right thing. Knowing what the lighting was going to be like made me focus like a laser beam. The dress couldn't be black, for one thing, and cheap tarty dresses are frequently black.

Hot pink worked, though. The one I eventually selected was polyester knit with no sleeves, a skirt just long enough to be street-legal, a built-in shelf bra, and no back to speak of. It had a high, choker neckline covered with pink crystals, with a thin clear-plastic strap across the back. So it was actually pretty secure, even though it looked like it would fall apart at a harsh word. Best of all, it was only fifty bucks.

I had to get shoes, too. By this time I was getting into the spirit of it and, I must confess, was thinking I could wear this to go dancing. Because by now I was thinking if Detective Cutie didn't ask me out by the end of the run, I was probably going to ask him. And while these particular shoes were to serve a specific, if hypothetical, purpose, I had to assume that I would be keeping them post-show. So I wasn't about to get some cheap crappy pair.

Given that, can I really be blamed for making a beeline for the hot-pink satin, ankle-strap, peep-toe sandals with crystals, and a heel perfect for dancing? They only cost five times as much as the dress.

I got back to the house around three and found Red champing at the bit to go get his car. I nobly refrained from asking why he couldn't have had Lesley take him to the garage, just bit my tongue and dropped him off.

Then I hurried back to the house to complete my evening's preparations. Director-wear: check. Tramp-wear: check. Makeup kit: check. Bag, phone, wallet: check. I was carrying a bigger bag than usual, which is saying something. This one needed to accommodate the dress (which rolled up to about the size of a water bottle) and the shoes (which were wrapped in a kitchen towel) as well as the makeup kit and everything else that I normally hauled around.

I was still hoping I wouldn't need to go on. If Susan didn't show, I'd have Prologue through Scene 4 to get into character. It would have to be enough.

X. Ysidro

First thing in the morning I checked in with forensics. They confirmed the pill bottle was an unintelligible mess of smudges, as I'd expected.

They also confirmed that five of the six sets of prints I'd collected from the theater were not matches to the prints of interest. That was good news for Matamoros, Garcia, Hidalgo, Loving, and Jackson – not that they would ever know.

The set of prints I took from Redding's shoes, though, told us all we really needed to know. When I opened up the email from Downtown and found reports of witnesses to the crosswalk push and the theater exit, I knew we had enough.

I double-checked the case log against the electronic file. Every interview had included the standard cautions. Every phone interview had included the notice of recording. My team's report on physical investigations at the West/Song house and theater was textbook. We were as clean as we could be. Warrants were sworn out, and Washington and Muñoz were sent out to make the arrest.

Half an hour later I got a call. "Boss, she's not home."

"Try with Marco Hidalgo. Don't call ahead."

"What are we, rookies? On our way."

She wasn't there, either. Now we had the prospect of staking out both locations all day, or planning to catch up with her at the theater. I took it to my commander. "A guy who works at El Pollo Loco saw the push. He'd been taking out the trash and was going back into the restaurant."

"And the day before?"

"Parking lot attendant sees Redding exiting the theater by the alley between eight and eight-fifteen. He noticed her because, well, she's noticeable."

The commander looked at some of my photos. It seemed no one had ever explained to Redding that if you have to wear shorts under it, the dress is not long enough. He nodded. "You think she would ditch the show?"

"Not really, no. I think she's obsessed with it actually, and wouldn't be surprised if she's planning to take another crack at somebody."

"Who would be the most likely target?"

"Since she didn't really get anywhere with the boyfriend, I think she might go for the young lady playing the ingénue."

"The what?"

I laughed. "Young girl singer. Redding is the understudy for the part."

"Okay. You've gotten to know these people pretty well?"

"As much as I could in four days."

"What's your play?"

"Put protective coverage on Cameron Monaghan, eyes on Redding's place, and if she doesn't go home show up at the theater and make the arrest."

"How many people you need?"

"If the budget will cover it I'd like to have Muñoz and Washington for the theater, a uniform at Redding's place, and a uniform for Monaghan."

"Okay. I'll back you. Go and set it up."

"Yes, sir." I called my team back. When they arrived we went through a basic plan of action. Then I pulled in the uniforms to send over to Monaghan's and Redding's apartments, and had Muñoz call Monaghan to let her know what was up while Washington called Redding's employer to suggest we would like a call if she showed up there. Once that was taken care of, we needed to start interviews over the crosswalk incident. We split up the list three ways, and got to our phones.

I took Hidalgo. After a couple of reassuring non-questions, I asked, "What time did you leave the theater last night, Marco?" He didn't know I'd been there, after all. But he told the truth about that.

"About twenty past eleven. We'd done a short piece of the show over again because Tanith wanted to try re-ordering two scenes."

"Oh yeah? How did that go?"

"Went fine. It was smoother the new way, fewer people to move back and forth."

"So did you go out with anybody?"

"Felipe and I spoke with Tanith, and I think pretty much everybody else was gone before we left. Felipe was going over to the parking lot, I went down Broadway to get something to eat."

"Not to El Pollo Loco?"

He laughed. "Once a day is enough."

"So you didn't see who Mr. Matamoros might have caught up with?"

"No."

"Was anyone waiting for you, to go get a bite? Miss Redding maybe?"

"No, I didn't see her when I went out."

"You didn't see her at all last night?"

"Not once rehearsal was over." More nerves in his voice.

"She didn't stay with you last night?"

"No." Voice getting higher.

"You guys have a fight?"

"No!"

"You sure? Why did Miz Salazar ask to talk to you and Mr. Matamoros?"

"Ah shit, man, give me a break." It was almost a wail.

"Mr. Hidalgo," I said pretty sharply, "Billy West is dead. This is a murder investigation. If you don't want to have this conversation on the phone with me, you can come in to the station and have it with me and your attorney. But we are going to have this conversation."

I could hear him breathing, could tell he was stressed. I gave him a few seconds to pull himself together.

"Tanith called me out for fouling Felipe's exit. I was distracted, and yeah, Susan and I had a fight. During intermission. She told me how disappointed she was that I wasn't trying harder to move up in the show. I told her that's not how it worked. You move up from one show to the next, not from one rehearsal to the next. She wouldn't listen."

"Thanks, Marco. That's all for now." I hung up. I looked up to see Teresa hanging over my cube's wall. "What's up?"

"Miss Monaghan says she saw Susan Redding leaving the group with Jenny Wilson last night, at the crosswalk. Monaghan was halfway up the block going to her car but turned around when she heard the horns and stuff. Saw Redding booking it down Third in the other direction. Or, in her words, 'clomping as fast as she could clomp in those ridiculous shoes.'"

"Well, what do you know."

Sam walked up then. "People have some interesting things to say this morning."

"What's new?"

"Miss Wilson says she had to take her sides away from Redding last night."

"Her what?"

"Her script."

"When was this?"

"Right before Act II started. Wilson was downstairs to do a costume change before she went on, looked for her script – just for reassurance, she says – and Redding had it."

"I really don't like that girl," said Teresa. I knew she meant Redding.

"Me neither." I looked up at Sam. "Anything from the canvass?"

"I want to say yes, but nothing solid. A yard worker half a block away says he saw a young lady – his words – walking away from the Salazar house mid-afternoon. Cutoff shorts and long bleached hair, he said. He does several houses on the block, so he's pretty familiar with the regulars. Says he couldn't ID the face but it wasn't a resident, at least not any of those he knows."

"Okay. Well, it's better than nothing, so thanks."

We were doing a split shift to minimize the overtime, so I went home after that and did another quick workout, took a shower, decided what to wear. Opening night was kind of a big thing, but I thought probably not a tuxedo thing. (Yeah, I have a tuxedo. I moonlight as security for the red carpet sometimes.) So I went with my favorite jacket, houndstooth check in gold and black, over a black sport shirt and slacks. Just in case, I wore shoes that I could run in.

XI. Tanith

Show time was eight o'clock, call time was seven. Of course I got to the theater early. Friday rush hour was not to be trifled with. And also I wanted to check out the box office and concessions setups.

"I am so glad I hired you guys," I said after looking everything over. "This looks spectacular." The lobby had a dry service bar and FOH (the name of the company; it stood for Front of House) had worked at the Million Dollar before, so they'd known exactly what to bring.

They had a pair of four-foot glass-fronted refrigerators flanking the theater's glass case, with bottled water, soft drinks, beer, and single-serving screw-top wine bottles. Coolers behind the case were chilling down additional stock.

In the case they had a good selection of sweet and salty snacks, plus a display of the souvenir gear. Finally, they had two sales kiosks set up, each in between a refrigerator and the case, so the cashiers could see anything being taken out of the refrigerator but also get stuff out of the case or do re-stocking. Smart.

Their cashiers were wearing show tee shirts with jeans and black change aprons. The box-office cashier had a show tee shirt on as well. I was thrilled, frankly.

The site manager handed me a program and postcard. I'd already seen and proofed the electronic versions, but it was nice to hold them in my hand. The postcards were hot off the press, with the web address

133

for the show's YouTube channel. "Your first show, right?" she said.

"The first that's all mine," I said.

"I watched the numbers online, they look good. Tell everybody to break a leg."

"Thanks." We shook hands and I went on in. I fully expected the theater to feel different tonight, and it did.

An empty theater has a certain personality; it's invariably kind of sleepy and morose. A theater with a show-in-progress shows signs of waking up. And a theater on opening night can either fight you or make things easy for you. This particular theater had an atmosphere of ... I can only describe it as conspiratorial glee.

How many shows had premiered here, over the past nine decades? I could only guess. But I had a feeling that the theater wanted us to succeed. Maybe that's just crazy showbiz wishful thinking. I don't believe so.

I remembered a show I'd done in a small theater up in Hollywood. It got used pretty much constantly, over three hundred nights a year, and it felt tired and cranky and, on opening night, hostile. Like, why don't you people just go away. Windows had broken, doors had stuck, toilets had clogged, lights had blown out – it was freaky.

The Million Dollar felt like, this is gonna be fun.

I went to my place at the tech box, set down my souvenirs, and then continued through to the stage and downstairs to hang up my just-in-case costume. I'd brought (also rolled up in my satchel) a lightweight garment bag with my name prominently Sharpied all over it, and hung the dress inside that, with the shoes tucked into the bottom corners. If Lesley asked I'd tell her it was for after the show – which might even be true. She came in while I was looking around. "Hey, boss. How's the nerves?"

"Don't ask. Did you see the lobby?"

"Yeah, it looks great, doesn't it?"

"If anybody asks, tell them the show is going to make sure everybody gets a tee shirt," I said.

"Awesome." Lesley, like the rest of us, had a collection of show tee shirts.

"You got everything you need?"

She looked around the dressing room. "Everything but actors."

"Any minute now." I headed back upstairs, checked the makeup room (clean for now), and then went to the back door. I cracked it open and stuck my head out into the alley. I was looking down – looking for Edgar – but I had the distinct impression that a person had just ducked back out of the alley into the narrow evacuation passage between the theater building and its neighbor. It gave me the creeps, and Edgar was nowhere in sight. I hoped he was okay.

Closing the door, I glanced at my wristwatch. It was almost seven. I went to the bathroom, then back out to the house to take up my position at the tech box. I passed Kevin on the way; we exchanged waves.

Yoshi, Brad, and Valerie were all there getting set up. Within the next five minutes Red, Tony, Jenny, and Liz came in. Close behind were Cameron, Lily, Felipe, and Miranda. The showgirls all trooped in together ("We carpooled"), followed by Dexter and then Marco. Then it looked like the volunteers had come in a van, because all nine came in as a group.

"We didn't want to take up all the parking," said Anthony as they passed. "So we borrowed Jerry's SUV."

"Thanks guys," I said. I checked my list. The only people I hadn't seen come in were Victor Garcia and Susan Redding. I fretted, gave it till seven-fifteen, and then stood up. "I'm taking a lap," I said to whoever was listening, and went out to the lobby.

I had a good reason: I'd forgotten to tell the box office to hold a ticket for Sid. But I also wanted to look for Susan and Victor. I was momentarily distracted by the line at the box office. It looked like some of the favors I'd called in (the ones involving 'please tell everybody you know') were paying off. The doors were open for the audience now, and people were starting to come in.

No sign of the missing persons, though. I went upstairs to the mezzanine and eyeballed the bathrooms. Nothing. Nobody in the balcony yet. Back downstairs. I remembered I was holding my walkie, and buzzed Kevin. "Hey Kev. Everything cool?"

"Everything's cool."

I changed frequencies. "Lesley?"

"Yeah?"

"I haven't seen Susan come in. Is she there?"

"Yeah, she's here."

Oh. Well, maybe I missed her.

"But where the hell is Victor?"

My heart lurched and I thought, *Shit.* "Kevin!"

"Yeah?"

"Have you heard from Victor?"

"Uh ... no."

"Me either. Can you give him a call?"

"Will do."

At seven forty-five we still had no word from Victor and my head was about to explode. I called a quick powwow. "Red, we don't know where Victor is. I need you to prep for Ivory. Marco, I'll need you as Mickey. So you're up in the prologue. Are you okay with the lines?"

"Yes, ma'am."

"Get into that glen plaid that Lesley found for you."

"Yes, ma'am."

"Dexter, can you take the Henchman?"

"Sure, Tanith."

"You're the best. We'll just have to lose the extra customer and Waiter 2. Go over the lines, okay? And think mean."

He laughed, looking nothing like an evil Henchman, and then tried on a scowl.

"Perfect, keep that." I patted him on the back and sent him away. Kevin and I looked at each other. "I have to make a phone call."

"It'll be okay, Tanith. You had all that coverage for a reason."

I shook my head and stepped back to the right wing. I could hear the commotion from the dressing room; people were excited, and probably also speculating about Victor. I pulled out my phone to call the one person I could think of who might actually be able to help me find out what was going on.

Sid picked up immediately. "You okay, Tanith?"

I was not too freaked out to notice that again he asked if I, personally, was okay. "I'm missing my Ivory."

"Shit," he said sincerely, and I fell a little bit in love. "Everybody else here?"

"Yes. Everybody. Red's getting in costume for Ivory, Marco's taking Mickey, and Dexter's taking the Henchman. Is there any way you could, you know ... ?"

"I'll make a couple of calls and get back to you." He disconnected and I just stood there, phone in one hand and walkie in the other, telling my brain to knock it off with the worst-case scenarios.

Kevin called the cast up to the stage at five till eight. Red was in costume, including the makeup that made him look older, skeevier, and a hell of a lot meaner. Still hunktastic, because the part required attractiveness, but in an overtly dangerous way. His physical presence was simply too different to play Ivory the same way Victor did. I wished I'd taken time to rehearse him in that role during the week. He was staring at me like 'what a fucking mess' and it was all I could do not to say that out loud.

Kevin said a few words that confirmed what was going on. I scanned all the faces and nobody looked guilty. Someone was a better actor than I'd thought.

I managed to give a short pep talk and then called places.

XI. Ysidro

I sent a text to Muñoz asking her to get on the Garcia problem and stay on it. She was covering the Third Street side of the building, back at the corner of the alley with a view of the back exit; Washington was outside up at the front. The plan, once we knew Redding was here, was to converge at the end of Act I and make the arrest at intermission, when audience movement would cover up any disruption. If any of us saw Redding trying to leave before then, of course, we'd make the collar then. This whole Garcia thing was a significant complication.

I switched my phone to vibrate as the overture started. The audience rustled and murmured and slowly quieted down. The curtain went up to show Wilson and Hidalgo onstage.

First scene change, blackout on stage. Lights up on the Blue Note set. Miranda Parker started to sing. I couldn't concentrate on the music. I'd asked for a seat in the back row on the aisle. Kept scanning the audience, not sure what I was looking for.

Dialogue scene, social dancers doing their stuff. Then the showgirls came on for their first number. My phone buzzed in my pocket.

Thanks to my position and the hot stuff onstage, I got out to the lobby without receiving a single dirty look. The text message from Muñoz said *Garcia's here. Long story.* I copied it to Tanith immediately. Looking through the porthole of the aisle door, I saw her jump a little as she got the message. She read it and I saw her shoulders relax. She lifted the walkie and spoke.

139

I made it back inside as the showgirls were finishing. Another dialogue scene. Then Ivory ... and there he was. Not in costume, but with such a predatory expression on his face that I thought probably no one would notice what he was wearing. With Dexter Parker as the Henchman, and a Susan Redding who looked the way you would imagine a mouse looks right before a snake grabs it. She gave her lines like a sleepwalker.

Garcia smiled at her in this negligent way, looking at her sideways as if he wasn't sure she was worth the trouble, but since she was here he might as well put her to some use. Then he went into his song, and I swear the temperature in the theater dropped five degrees.

How to describe it? The song was this doo-wop kind of ballad, swingy, not threatening at all. But the hair on the back of my neck went up, and I actually saw the woman seated in front of me shiver.

There was a roar of applause at the end of the song, and I saw Tanith bounce a little. When the commotion died down, Garcia nudged Redding through to the end of the scene, as the Eighties roofie equivalent kicked in. Parker scooped her up and carried her offstage. I beat it out to the lobby again, phone in hand. I watched through the porthole in the auditorium door as the lights went down for the scene change. "Sam, you there?"

"Right here."

"I'll cover the interior, okay. I'm gonna tag Muñoz and have her hold position. You go and cover the other side, where that evac passage is. There's that other exit, I don't want Redding getting out that way."

Lights were up on the police-station office set. Rogers and Hidalgo.

"Got it. Still going to put the bag on her at Intermission?"

"That's the plan. I'm going to tag the director and see if she has someone who can sit on Redding inside."

A quick text to Tanith: *Where's Warner*. Had to wait a couple of minutes. Lights were down for the set change, and then we were back at the Blue Note for Monaghan's first song.

Buzz. *Backstage ready for Waiter 2*.

Can he sit on Redding?

I'll tag him.

More waiting as she lifted the walkie. Dialogue scene. Rogers' solo. Finally, a buzz. *Yes and Lesley will cover when he's on in Sc.12.*

Good.

The showgirls were doing their second number. I slipped back inside to take my seat. Scene change, to the street; then the café, with Warner and Hidalgo on with Wilson and Rogers; then the street again for the Act I finale. I managed to scoot all the way down the aisle to the emergency door during the brief blackout.

Big applause at the end of the act. The house lights came up and the audience started doing what it does. I jogged up the steps to the stage, pushed through the curtain, and headed down to the dressing room, where I found complete pandemonium.

Warner was kneeling in front of Hayes, who was sitting on a folding chair with her hand to her head. Everyone else was milling around. I used my crowd-control voice. "Okay, everybody, I need you to settle down. What happened here?"

Everybody turned to look at me, with varying degrees of surprise. I didn't see Susan Redding anywhere, and I started to get a very bad feeling.

"Susan clocked Lesley and took off," said Warner. "She was out almost cold when I got down here."

"Did someone call 911?"

"She hit me with her fucking shoe," mumbled Hayes. I saw the ugly patent-leather stripper shoe, under the counter six feet away.

"Yeah, I called," said Warner.

"Good job," I said. I looked around at the now-silent group. Washington was standing at the back of the room, Muñoz on the stairs. "You all have the right to know we have a warrant for Susan Redding's arrest for the murder of Billy West. If any of you should see her at any time, do not approach her but immediately call 911 or find a policeman. We're putting out an APB right now."

Washington had his phone out before I finished speaking.

"I'll stay down here with Miz Hayes until the EMTs arrive. I'd recommend all of you make your changes for Act II and then just hang tight. We need to sweep the theater and make sure Redding isn't still here somewhere."

Garcia asked, "Are we supposed to go on with the show?"

"I'm going to call in some reinforcements for the property search and we're going to try to make it as non-disruptive as possible. Miz Hayes, is there any chance you saw which way Redding went?"

"She went up left," she said groggily.

"Who would have been in the left wing?"

"We were up left," said one of the showgirls. "But those stairs, ugh. We always come across the stage after curtain and go down to the dressing room on the right."

Another showgirl added, "Kevin was over there. Where is he?"

I exchanged a look with Muñoz. She disappeared up the stairs. "We'll figure it out."

My phone buzzed. *WTF IS GOING ON*. From Tanith, of course. I called her back on the voice line, catching myself one second before using her first name. "Miz Salazar, have you seen Mr. Jackson?"

"He went tearing out the Third Street door after someone, right as intermission started, it's a mob scene in here, what is going – "

I cut her off, no time to be polite. "Can anyone get back in through that side door?"

"No."

"Please go into the lobby and watch for him. Call me if you see him. I have to make another call."

"Okay." She clicked off.

I called the Downtown division and explained our need for support. Fortunately it was a quiet night and they were able to scramble some uniforms. I thought they wouldn't find anything, and it turned out I was right.

About a half hour later, I found out Jackson came panting back in during intermission, with news I really didn't want to hear.

XII. Tanith

Kevin told me he'd seen Susan bolting up from the left stairs and that she'd cut across the stage almost before the curtain was down. He'd followed her out the side door almost by instinct.

I threw discretion out the window and told him everything, at least everything I could get out in a minute or less. He wasn't surprised. "I knew something was up. When she saw Victor she looked ready to pass out. She ran down Third and cut into the alley behind the Bradbury building," he said. "I knew the cops were here, so I figured I'd better just come back and let the pros handle it."

"As far as I know, we're clear to keep going. Sid said he and his team would try to keep things quiet."

"We'd better connect with the cast." We started worming through the crowd in the lobby. Friends were there, of course, and we had to smile and say "Hey!" and make we're-still-working faces and just not stop. It looked like extending the intermission by fifteen minutes would be a good idea. When we got inside I leaned over to ask Brad to make an announcement or two, he nodded, and we proceeded up to the stage.

Onstage, half the cast was milling around. The emergency exit was propped open and I could see emergency lights flashing out in the alley. "What's up?"

"The EMTs are here to get Lesley," someone said.

"Lesley?! What happened?"

"Susan hit her and ran out."

"Son of a bitch!" I went over to the alley door. They already had Lesley out on a gurney in the alley. She was complaining, so I figured she wasn't at death's door, but I called across to her anyway. "Lesley! You okay?"

"They've got me strapped in like I don't know what. My head hurts, but my neck ain't broke." She put on a woebegone hillbilly accent and I gave thanks for my crazy friends.

"Then I guess we won't have to shoot you after all," I drawled. "Call me when they let you, okay?"

"You betcha."

I went back inside and shushed the gang. Kevin had brought everyone up from downstairs. "Okay, settle down, everybody. This is sure not the normal opening night, huh?"

Murmurs of agreement.

"Here's the good news. Lesley is okay, Victor is okay, and everybody else is okay. We're going to let the police worry about Susan. Until further notice, it's on with the show."

Kevin said, "The new scene order went fine. Has anybody got any questions or concerns about Act II?"

A chorus of Nope and It's fine and We're good. I heard Brad make the fifteen-minute announcement.

"I have to go back out to the house, but you've got Kevin and Red and the LAPD. Don't be afraid to ask any of them for whatever." I must have seemed steadier than I felt; everyone looked reassured, and ready to proceed. Before I went back out, I took a tour of the whole backstage area. Everything looked normal. I wondered where Edgar was, but there wasn't time to check on him.

Why would I be thinking about a cat at a time like this? Because of all the things I was trying to juggle, he was the simplest. I think that's what it came down to.

As I passed by the holding area on my way back out, I saw Sid coming in from the alley. We stopped and looked at each other. For a terrible, embarrassing few moments I thought I was going to cry. Then I took a deep breath, nodded to him, and continued on.

Act II went perfectly.

It was weird. I knew there were cops combing the dressing room and crypt and wings and who-knew-what-else. And I knew that murderous little twat was somewhere out in L.A., maybe getting away for good. But somehow I managed to box everything else out and just watch.

Had I cast just the perfect people, or was I a really good director? I couldn't say, but I was truly, deeply satisfied. Cameron got a moment of silence and then a long ovation after her third number. Victor'd gotten the same after his second. Some kind of energy was loose in the house and everyone there seemed to be riding a wave.

This wasn't 'Cabaret.' It wasn't 'Les Miserables.' It was a brand-new, untried little show, with a writer/director nobody'd ever really noticed, and a cast of people mostly known only to other actors in L.A., in an ancient theater.

But for a few minutes, something magic happened.

After the show, it took me a long time to get clear of the house and get onstage. Kevin had the cast assembled. I didn't have a clue what to say. Finally I opened my arms, shrugged, and said, "Seven thirty tomorrow, everybody. Great job tonight."

Kevin sent everybody down to change. Victor hung back. "I wanted to tell you what happened, why I was late," he said.

He looked tired. I could relate. "Have you spoken to Detective Palacio?"

"No, not yet. He's been kind of in and out."

"Can you hang for a few, wait for him? That way you'll only have to tell it once." I indicated the chairs in the dancers' holding area.

"Sure, okay."

Kevin said, "You want me to hang out?"

"Yeah, if you can."

"I'll go get us something from concessions."

"Excellent idea," I said gratefully. He loped off up the aisle to the lobby, where FOH was closing up. He caught them in time, because he was back in a few minutes with four cold beers. Sid joined us just as Kevin was opening the bottles with a churchkey from the set's bar.

"Thanks," said Sid, taking an offered bottle.

"No nonsense about being on duty?" I said.

"I'm relieved. My commander's putting Detective Washington in charge of the case from here on out."

"What? Why?"

"Poor judgement. I should have collared Redding as soon as she came offstage. We knew she was getting violent."

"It was, like, ten minutes," I protested. "And the show was going on. How were you supposed to get backstage?"

"I should have sent Detective Muñoz down from her station to take care of it. Miz Hayes wouldn't have gotten hit, and Redding wouldn't have gotten away."

"Well, shit," I said. Sid laughed. I did a 'what the fuck' thing with my hands.

"Washington's a good cop," he said. "He'll handle it."

I was glad he trusted his team, but I was still annoyed. I wanted *my* cop on the case. "So, Victor wanted to tell us why he was late. Can you take his statement?"

"Let me just clear it with Sam." He set down the still-full bottle and stepped aside, phone in hand. Evidently his partner didn't have a problem, because Sid laughed a couple of times and then came back over. "Okay. Remember the standard cautions, Mr. Garcia?"

"Couldn't forget them if I tried."

"I'm gonna record this, okay?"

"Sure."

"All right, ready to go."

"It was a bomb threat," Victor said flatly. "Phoned into my building at five-thirty. LAPD's bomb squad probably has all their side of the story. But basically, the whole parking garage was locked down and the building was evacuated."

"Where did they put you? You got here at, what, eight-fifteen?"

"About that. And I'm probably in some kind of trouble, because I didn't get permission to leave. My phone was in my apartment, my car was in lockdown, they had us corralled in the parking lot of the building across the street. But I had my wallet and I just walked away. Got a taxi and came down here."

Sid asked a couple of clarifying questions about times and places, then turned off the recorder. "That should be all we need."

"Well Victor," I said, "I'm really glad you made it because you were phenomenal. Thanks for making the effort." I hoped my voice managed to convey 'because if you hadn't this show would be toast.' It might have been a slight exaggeration, but only slight. I'd seen the panic in Red's eyes at the prospect of taking the part. He could have boxed it out, but with five minutes to prepare? Ugh.

Victor's smile said he understood. "Thanks. I don't know how much of that was acting tonight."

"If anyone asks, I'll tell them all of it."

"I'll make sure there's no trouble," said Sid. "We know some guys on the bomb squad."

"Thanks," Victor said again, and stood up. "Do you think … I don't want to sound like a wimp, but is it safe to go home?"

"Personally," said Sid, "I'd prefer it if nobody was alone. Your building is secure?"

"Yeah, it is. Coded entrance and a doorman."

"Let's make sure your doorman has a picture of Redding. I'll text one to you. If you want somebody with you, give them a call now."

"Okay. I have someone I can call."

"You can go now, if you want." Sid stood, offering his hand, and Victor shook it. I thought, very inappropriately, that they'd make great screen partners, like Claude Rains and Humphrey Bogart. Too bad Sid wasn't in show business. Too bad all this crap was actually happening in real life.

"I can give you a lift," said Kevin. "I live up your way." He'd finished his beer. None of us said anything about drinking and driving.

"Great, thanks."

"I'll keep you updated," I promised. Victor leaned in for a hug, and Kevin gave me a wave as they left the stage.

"What. A. Night," I said, plopping back down on my chair. Sid laughed ruefully, still standing. I handed him the bottle of beer. He drank some of it this time. "They seriously took you off the case?"

"Not off the case, just off as team leader. And it's the right call. I lost my focus ... was thinking how to make sure your show didn't get messed up, and should have been thinking how to get Redding in the bag."

"I'm sorry." It was totally inappropriate to be pleased that he'd been thinking more about me than about his job. Tsk tsk, bad Tanith.

"Don't worry about it. We'll get her. And it was a great show," he said. "Who will play the Girl tomorrow?"

"Me, I guess," I said. "Good thing I already bought a dress." It was such a great exit line, I tipped up my bottle and drained it. Then I thought hell, I have to drive home. Sid was laughing. "I have to go ask Red to drive me home now."

"I'll let you get to it." He was still standing there when I headed down to the dressing room.

"Hey big guy," I said. Red was sitting in the middle of the deserted dressing room, which was a complete mess. "I might have just guzzled down a bottle of beer."

"Where's mine?" He leaned back in the totally inadequate chair.

"You don't get one. You have to drive. Oh *shit* what about Lesley? You don't think they'll keep her overnight, do you?"

He rubbed his hands over his face. Fortunately he'd taken off his makeup. "I'll take care of it. You stop for a cheeseburger ASAP, and take surface streets."

"It'll take all night," I complained, but it was the best solution. I touched him on the shoulder, then bent and kissed his cheek. "You're a rock star. Thanks." He waved me away.

XII. Ysidro

My night was far from over. Washington oversaw the clearing of the building, then sent the Downtown uniforms off. He sent me to find the theater's security office and ask about extra locks for the doors. The security guy produced chains and padlocks which were duly attached to the three doors at the back, and promised to chain the lobby doors on his way out (as he usually did).

I had a look around the alley for Edgar before we locked up that door, but didn't see him. I hoped nothing bad had happened.

Redding's car was still in the Third Street lot. The Downtown force had booted it and posted a BOLO, but she could have taken a taxi anywhere, or a bus, or even the train.

Muñoz had left a half hour earlier – with Marco Hidalgo, in handcuffs. Turns out he had let Redding in through the evac passage door at about seven-thirty.

By the time Washington and I got back to our station, Hidalgo was more than ready to spill all his beans. It wasn't so much a matter of getting him to talk, as getting him to shut up. Unfortunately, what he had to say wasn't terrifically useful.

He swore he didn't know where she'd spent the day, or the night before, but he told us she basically lived out of her car and had lots of friends to crash with.

"How did she make all these friends, Marco?" Sam asked. "We can't find a single person who likes her."

"She can be nice," he said feebly.

"When she wants something from you, right?" Teresa said. "How many of these friends are there, Marco? Eight? Twenty? Or is it more like two?"

"I don't know them, okay? I've only known her for a month and a half."

We hit him with question after question. "You never met up with anybody? She didn't talk about anybody?"

"How about someone from one of those video shoots she did, she never mentioned anything?"

"Why'd she keep that apartment?"

"Was someone else living there with her?"

"Was it an illegal sublet, is that it?"

"Was she involved with drugs?"

"Was she turning tricks?"

We hammered away and finally got the picture we'd come to expect. Marginal talent, marginal jobs, just enough money to keep up appearances but only by living pretty much in the gray. The apartment was more of a squat than a sublet – the legal tenant had sublet, illegally, to a person who had then invited three others to share. They were each paying about five hundred dollars a month.

Redding's job as a waitress had provided her with free food most days. The clothes and shoes, we were assuming, were mostly shoplifted. We were getting a warrant for the apartment and expected nothing much from the search except to cause a lot of trouble for the legal tenant.

By the time we figured we'd squeezed Hidalgo dry, it was almost three in the morning and we were all pretty fried. We put him in a holding cell for the rest of the night, expecting to cut him loose in the morning.

153

I had a conference with my commander at nine. It went as well as could be expected, which is to say the ass-chewing was about a seven on a one-to-ten scale. As I was limping back to my desk I saw Washington, leaning against the wall with a face that said the day wasn't getting better. "What's up?" I said.

"Hidalgo's apartment building suffered a fire last night."

I stared at him, blinked, took a breath. "Anybody hurt?"

"No, thanks to functional smoke alarms, charged extinguishers, and some amateur fire-setting."

"No doubt it's arson, huh."

"Couldn't have been more obvious. Kerosene, rags, right inside Hidalgo's door."

"Jeez." I did a double-take. "Wait a second, you said *inside* the door?"

"Yep. So we need to wake up Mr. Hidalgo and ask him if he gave Redding a copy of his key."

He said he hadn't, but he also said he'd left her at the apartment one day while he went to work. Which is pretty much inviting someone to copy keys as well as to steal anything you have that isn't nailed down.

"Did you ever find anything missing after Susan stayed with you?" I asked.

"No. I helped her out with money a couple of times. She didn't take anything." Dude looked completely downtrodden.

"Your apartment's a crime scene, Marco," Sam said. "You can't go home today. You have somewhere to go?"

"I can go to my gym, I guess," he said forlornly.

"You have your phone, right? Some money?"

"I'll be okay. I just ... can't believe she would do all this. I can't believe anyone would."

"Welcome to the real world, Marco."

"I've got to call Tanith. Apologize. See if she wants me to come tonight."

I got him some coffee and a danish from the vending machine in the canteen, and let him get to it.

I was technically off the clock but my commander wasn't saying anything about seeing my face at the station. I hung around till Washington got his warrant and headed off with a uniform to search Redding's apartment. Then I reviewed the report the bomb squad had sent over from the Garcia incident the day before.

There was no evidence there had ever been an actual explosive, I was relieved to find. It sounded like she had called in the threat for the sole purpose of keeping Garcia out of the theater – which had almost worked. The building's front desk didn't have an automatic recording function on the incoming line, but the day security guy confirmed the threat had come from a woman. First time that had ever happened, he was quoted as saying. What, a bomb threat? No, that it was a woman.

Way to bust the profile, Redding.

I was almost impressed at the range of crimes she'd embarked upon. The more I thought about it, the more I was finding it hard to believe this was all new. There had to be something in her history, something aside from that 'freak accident' that, apparently, no one had thought to investigate.

Ultimately, of course, it didn't matter. With all the witnesses and the physical evidence, the prosecutor was going to be pretty happy with this one. Once we brought her in.

A uniform came in. "That big dude is asking if there's any way someone could get him to his car."

"I'll take him."

I sent Washington a text to let him know I was going home via the Third Street parking lot downtown, but to call me if he needed extra hands. Then I collected Hidalgo, and headed out.

We didn't say much on the drive. As I pulled in to the parking lot Hidalgo heaved a sigh of relief that his car was still there. "What're you going to do now, Marco?"

"Go to the gym. I've got a change of clothes in the car. Then I guess I'll go to work, I was scheduled today from one to five." He worked at Best Buy.

"Did you talk to Miz Salazar?"

"Yeah," he said on a sigh. "She said I couldn't be held responsible for somebody else being crazy, but she was going to keep Dexter in the Henchman part, but Red as Mickey and Waiter 1. So I'll be doing the customer and Waiter 2."

"Better than nothing," I said. He nodded sadly, and got out of the car. I watched as he went over to the attendant, explained, argued, and finally forked over what was probably close to fifty dollars. The mean part of me thought he was getting off pretty lightly; the lot was posted for no overnight parking and the attendant could have had him towed.

As he drove away, I realized I was a little light-headed. Little sleep and no breakfast will do that to you. I decided to park, and walk down to the Nickel Diner.

And maybe, on the way back, take a swing through the alley behind the theater and check on Edgar. As it turned out, that was a good idea; when I got there with my to-go cup of water and parcel of bacon omelet, I didn't see him ... but I heard him.

As I walked down the alley, there was no sign of him. Tanith had mentioned seeing him on the fire escape, so I looked up there. Then as I got close to the dumpster I said out loud, "Where you hiding, Edgar? Got you breakfast."

An agonized howl came from the dumpster, making me jump. I set down the water and the omelet, and opened both of the top panels. A wave of heat rolled out at me.

Edgar was crouched in a corner, near a tiny hole where rust had eaten away the container. It must have let in just a trickle of something close to fresh air. He was panting and wild-eyed, and when he saw me he howled again.

"I understand completely," I told him, and climbed in. Luckily there wasn't much in there, aside from a few stuffed black trash bags. I mean, if you're going to climb into a dumpster, this was the one to climb into. But still, it had that uniquely sharp and funky stink of decomposing food, stale beer, and body fluids.

I bent halfway down to Edgar, and he jumped right up to my chest. He was trembling. "Okay, buddy," I said. "Hang on." There was a little pile of rusty shreds in the corner, like he'd tried to claw the hole bigger. I held him tight.

With one hand securing the cat, I clambered back out. The sun was at an angle that left no shade in the alley except in the gap behind the dumpster, where the opened flaps created an awning. I set Edgar down there (detaching several claws from my shirt) and opened the cup of water. He immediately drank quite a lot.

Half a minute later he vomited. I squatted down and put my hand on his shoulders. He was hot to the touch, and shaking, but he started up a raspy purr. A minute or two later he tried again with the water. This time it stayed down. He nosed at the omelet, then looked up at me.

"I don't think I'd better leave you here, big guy," I said. I put the cap back on the water, scooped Edgar up in one arm and tucked the omelet under his paw, picked up the water and walked over to my car.

Once I had the engine running I turned on the air conditioning. There was a towel in the back seat and I put it on the passenger seat beside the cat, forming it into a little crescent around him. He crouched there, still trembling.

"You're going to be mad," I said, "but you're going to the vet."

He stared at me, communicating as clear as day 'life stinks,' and then gave a silent meow. It was the most pitiful thing I ever saw.

"I know, buddy," I said. "I know."

When I got to the VCA I wrapped Edgar up in the towel and carried him in. I set him on the counter and he stayed there while I answered questions and filled out forms. Then we went to sit down till a vet was free to see us. We didn't have to wait long.

"He's quite a looker," said the vet. "That's a really unusual coloring for a male cat. He might be sterile, or a hermaphrodite."

"Don't listen, Edgar," I said. The vet laughed.

"No, but see his face? That's what I call kitten face. Going by his teeth, he's probably about two years old. A tomcat by this age would usually have a really full face, like Marlon Brando as the Godfather."

"So that's why his eyes look so big."

"Right. He's a nice guy, isn't he?" She was stroking Edgar, who was purring again.

"Yeah, he is."

She gave me some pheromone spray to help Edgar settle in to my apartment, telling me to bring him back if he started marking, that he might need to be neutered after all. Then the service person made sure I had food, dishes, an emergency litter box, et cetera so I didn't have to stop at Petco on the way home.

And then I wrapped my cat back up, stuffed him in the cardboard VCA carrier, and we left. All the way back to my place I was wondering who could have shut him in the dumpster. I was also wondering if this was just one more shitty thing our fugitive might be responsible for. And why? Just to be shitty? Or had she seen me or Tanith interacting with the cat, and figured this was a way to distract us?

Had to admit, it worked. I was starting to revise my estimate of Redding's intelligence. After parking at my place, I called Washington to report this development. He didn't pick up, so I left a message and told him I'd write it up. I could just imagine his face when he heard it.

XIII. Tanith

The cops made sure that nobody went back to their car alone. Red and I walked out together after checking with the hospital. They wanted to keep an eye on Lesley for a couple more hours. He headed over there (via a drive-through, I was sure) to wait for her, and I went home (also via a drive-through). I was kind of numb, possibly from the beer but mostly from Too Much. Professionally the night had been a success, but that was zeroed out by the clusterfuck with Susan. It was impossible for me to blame Sid for that, though maybe I should have. In any case, once Red got Lesley home and we all finally went to bed, I switched off.

I didn't set my alarm, turned off my phone, did the Zzz-Quil thing, and still woke up at eight. I lay there for a long few minutes running through my repertoire of curses, but eventually had to concede that I might as well get up.

First: bathroom, and check on Lesley (still asleep). Second: coffee. Third: breakfast. Fourth: email. Wow, the email.

I read through all the messages, then took the better part of an hour to compose a note to the entire cast and crew. I reiterated that call time was seven-thirty and we were all systems go as far as the show went, but cautioned that the cops might be around again and that security on the building would be tighter. No one was to use the side doors or the rear exit unless the building was actually on fire (smiley face). I recommended Nicorette to the few smokers.

And I confirmed – after taking a break to confer with Red – the new casting. Right about the time that

I sent the message, Lesley came into my room. "You okay?" I said, giving her an assessing look.

"I'm okay. Little bit of headache."

"If you don't want to come to the theater tonight, I think we can manage."

"I'll let you know how I feel later on. Hungry now."

"Want me to fix you something?"

She smiled. "You don't have to do that."

"I feel responsible."

"It's okay." She patted me on the shoulder and went back out. I listened to her assembling a bowl of cereal, carrying it out to the dining room, going back for a cup of coffee. When the spoon started hitting the bowl I relaxed a little, and turned on my phone. It was well past noon by this time. There were over a dozen voice messages and twice as many texts to get through.

Most of them I'd disposed of via the email, but there was a message from Mom. And it suddenly occurred to me that what I most wanted right then was to talk to my Mom. So I called her back, and told her the whole long stupid story. We talked about Billy again, and cried a little bit over it again. I told her I felt responsible.

"Don't be ridiculous," she said, sniffling. "You were casting a musical, not a snuff film. And you got her name from me, so if it's anybody's fault it's mine."

I coughed out a laugh. "Okay. So if I'm ever casting anything again, all the gods forbid, please don't send me anybody who washed out of Idol."

"So what about this cat?" she said, changing the subject. Mom was a cat lady, she had three of her own

161

and fostered rescues. She'd been bugging me to adopt one for years.

"I may go back this afternoon to look for him."

"Do you think that's a good idea? What if that crazy girl is still hanging around down there? Shouldn't you go with somebody?"

"Maybe not, who knows, maybe so." Just then my phone buzzed to signal an incoming text. "Can you hang on for a sec, Mom?"

"Sure."

I read the text; it was from Sid. *Found Edgar, he's with me. More later.* I sent back a quick reply: *WTH happened?*

Then I clicked back over to Mom. "Crisis averted. The cute detective found the cat. I'm going to call him and get the story."

"Oh good. You do that. And I'll see you tomorrow."

"Okay Mom. Love you."

"Love you too."

I disconnected and immediately dialed Sid. He didn't pick up, annoyingly; so I left a message to call me, and then hung up again.

And I realized that what I really wanted now was a hard workout. Lesley was lying on her bed watching something on her laptop, Red was in the prop shop. I told them I was going to the gym, and went out.

Just for the record, I hate the gym. It's loud and smelly and gross. But living in the Valley, where on any given day there is only a two-hour window to do anything outside when the temperature and air quality are bearable, and that's usually the time when you have to be getting ready for work, a gym membership is an expense I file under 'utilities.'

My gym had a good weight room, a cardio center with tons of machines, a climbing wall, and a yoga studio. My routine was a warmup on the elliptical, then weights, then yoga. I was one of a few women who used the free weights, plus I used one of the weight machines to do pull-ups and hanging leg raises.

Since I wanted to get good and tired, I did the full routine plus some extra yoga – balances and back bends I often wimped out on. As I lay on the mat sweating, and letting my spine settle into its newly-straightened configuration, I started laughing.

Another woman – an actress I knew to say "hi" to - was in there and she looked at me questioningly. "I'm doing this show," I explained, "and I just had an idea for a rewrite." She nodded with complete comprehension, smiled, and went back to her sun salutes.

I showered, changed, and got my stuff together to go home. Before I went out to the car I checked my phone. Of course, I'd missed Sid's call back. But it was now almost four o'clock. Should I call him, or would I see him tonight? I realized I had no idea what was going on with the investigation. Would Sid even know, now that Detective Washington was playing the lead?

Obviously the cops had better things to do than feed me updates, but ... well, you know. Between the cat and the crazy person, I thought I needed to check in. So I sat on the wall under the pepper tree in the parking lot, and called. This time he picked up.

"Let me give you the rundown on the investigation," he said. "Arson at Hidalgo's building last night, nobody was hurt. No sign of Redding at her apartment or her workplace, and her car is still booted at the Third Street lot. We've checked in with all the key cast members and everyone is reporting as fine."

I took a moment to assimilate that, not even wanting to ask for more details about the arson, then said, "Well, that's all good. Are you guys going to be at the theater again tonight?"

"Downtown division still has a BOLO and there have been foot patrols around the theater area all day. It's our feeling that Redding may come back there."

"Do you think she's going to try something else?"

"Just to be on the safe side, we have to assume so. No sightings have been reported at Union Station or the airport. But we have an issue." He sounded annoyed.

I hoped it wasn't with me. "What?"

"There's been a little scuffle over turf. My commander has pulled his resources back to Van Nuys. So our team won't be assigned to the theater tonight. Downtown division is assigning coverage starting at six."

"What about you?"

"If I'm there, it's on my own time."

"Oh. Well." I couldn't think of anything to say, or rather the only things I thought of to say either weren't very polite, or were too close to begging. I wanted him to be there.

"Do you want me to be there? Remember it's my fault she's in the wind."

"Oh, fuck that," I said. "Yeah, I'd like you to be there. I'm sure the downtown cops are great, but I feel like you understand the show, and the theater, and ...

well, I'd just like you to be there. I'll hold a ticket for you again."

"No need to do that, I can hang backstage. I'd rather be back there anyway since Downtown may not have anybody inside except in the lobby."

"Okay. Great." I was trying not to let my voice show the extent of my relief. "Well, now that that's settled, what about Edgar?"

He told me the story, and I slipped a few more notches toward love. Also possibly hero-worship. The guy climbed into a dumpster to rescue a stray cat. That was above and beyond. My mother was going to adore him.

He wrapped up with, "He's okay. I took him to the VCA and got him checked out, picked up the stuff he needed. So he's with me here at home now."

"I want visitation privileges."

"No problem." The smile was back in his voice.

XIII. Ysidro

No, it was not a problem that Tanith had just invited herself over to my house. It was the opposite of a problem, frankly, aside from the fact that she was a witness in an active case. I didn't mention to her that I'd already had an email exchange with my landlord about the cat. My original lease stated 'no pets,' but I'd been in the condo for a long time, and I was renting from the owner and not a management company. I thought it was worth pushing the issue.

They huffed and puffed a little, then suggested a small rent increase. It had been a couple of years since they bumped it up, so I agreed. After that was all settled I looked at the cat. "You're an expensive little son of a gun."

He blinked at me. The VCA had run some blood tests to confirm that he didn't have any horrible disease. They'd given him a sponge bath, which I'm sure he needed. Anyway, he'd cooled off enough for a regular physical exam and once the lab results were in I expected to hear that he was a normal, healthy cat.

After getting home, he inspected the entire place while I checked and returned messages and emails. It felt weird not being on the case after the intensity of the past few days. It also felt weird knowing that the primary responsibility had been handed off to another station.

But I knew my commander had to account for every personnel hour, and thanks to my screw-up he was way over budget with nothing to show for it. Part of me hoped that Redding would show up and try something at the theater, and that I could put the bag on her. Even though I'd be technically off duty, Downtown would have a hard time justifying taking the collar off our station.

Politics, right?

Edgar seemed to have chosen a chenille pillow on my loveseat for a nap. I turned on the TV to keep him company while I went to take a shower.

My plan was to get down to the theater between seven and seven-thirty, let the Downtown personnel know I was there inside by the director's invitation, do a reconnaissance, and then settle in. By five-thirty I was getting dressed. Jeans, Nikes, a black tee shirt and a lightweight blazer to cover the holster and handcuffs. Badge clipped to the inside left front pocket. Extra ammo.

Way too early to leave, and a little too early to eat. I looked at the sleeping cat and woke up my phone. "Hey Ma. How you doin'?"

"I'm fine, nice to hear from you. What's the occasion?"

"I got a cat."

She laughed. "How did that happen?"

"He's been hanging around the alley behind this place that's involved in a case. Downtown. I was down there today and found somebody shut him in a dumpster."

"Oh, poor kitty! He's lucky you were there."

"Yeah, he would have cooked for sure if he'd been in there much longer. Anyway I thought you would get a kick out of that."

"You're right. Your dad always fussed at me for bringing home strays, but you should have seen him the last time one of ours died."

"Dad's as much of a sucker as you are."

"You too, sounds like. What does he look like?"

"He's a mess. I'll text you a picture."

"Okay. So when are you coming up to see us?"

"How's Thanksgiving? If I can get off the schedule."

"That would be great! You going to bring anybody?"

"I wouldn't count on it, but I'll let you know."

"Okay baby. You working tonight?"

"Yeah, sort of."

"Well, take care."

"I will. Say hi to Pop for me."

"I will. Love you."

"Love you too." After clicking off, I took a picture of Edgar – who cooperated by opening both green eyes just a little, making himself look thoroughly stoned – and sent it to Mom. A few seconds later she texted back: *LOL he's cute.* And I thought, yeah, he kind of was.

Then I sent the picture to Tanith, and sat around waiting for a reply, because that's basically where I was with her. It took a few minutes but she did write back. *Awww. Guess that's his pillow now.*

Fixed dinner, fed the cat, cleaned up the kitchen. Found myself talking to Edgar off and on. He occasionally chirped in reply. I'd grown up with relays of pets, but had never gotten one since I'd lived on my own. A serious girlfriend, for several years, had a couple of dogs and a cat; those had been my proxy pets. Now I wondered why I'd never adopted one. It was going to be nice to come home to a place that wasn't entirely empty.

At six-thirty my phone rang. It was Tanith. "I'm about to head downtown. Lesley doesn't feel up to going and I told her we could manage without her. Do you think it's safe to leave her here alone?"

"I think it probably is, but if someone could come over I'd feel better about it."

"Me too. I mean, that's what I thought. Okay, I'm going to call Uncle Kyong."

"Good idea."

"See you downtown." She clicked off.

And that meant it was time for me to get on the road too. I told Edgar not to worry, I'd be home later. He gave me a disapproving look and turned around to show me his butt. I laughed and went out.

Traffic in and around L.A. is never what you'd call light, but at least it was trouble-free today. I got downtown in twenty-five minutes and parked in the Third Street lot near the theater. Redding's car wasn't there. I asked the attendant if he knew anything about it. He said it had been towed earlier "and a couple of cops were here." So I figured it was now in impound, and wondered if she'd been picked up.

I checked in with Sam and he said, "Not as far as I know. Let me check with the station down there. They were supposed to keep us updated, and I never heard anything about moving the car."

"Maybe the parking lot management asked them to."

"Yeah, maybe. I'll let you know what I find out."

It was annoying, having the game of phone tag going on. The Downtown guys in the field would be relaying info back to their station, their front-desk staff there would relay it to our station, and the front-desk staff at our station would then pass it on to Sam. And he was, like me, technically off-duty. But when you're working a homicide, the official phone never gets turned off.

I flashed my badge to the box-office person (jumping the line forming outside) and the uniform stationed in the lobby, and walked on in to the theater. It was about seven-fifteen and Tanith was there with the other crew at the tech box. "Detective," she said, with the ghost of a smile. "Glad you could make it."

"Everything okay backstage?"

"Seems to be. We're just going over the cues and stuff. Kevin had to update his script again."

"What color did you use this time?" I asked him.

"Had to go to pink. That's a first," he said.

Tanith said, "Okay, guys. You've got everything you need, right?" They all indicated that they did. She nodded firmly and turned to me. She had her big satchel slung over her shoulder and her walkie in her hand. "Then I guess it's down to the dressing room for me. Kevin, please tag me at seven-forty if anyone hasn't come in. Gods forbid."

"Will do."

We both walked down the aisle, followed by arriving audience members. We left them at the front and mounted the steps to the stage.

XIV. Tanith

I expected Red to get to the theater by call time; he'd promised to wait at home until Uncle Kyong got there. Since the other crew were all out front, Sid and I were the first ones down to the dressing room. It was a still a mess, and would have to stay that way. The cops had taken everything from Susan's station.

"So, where do you think you want to hang out?" I asked Sid. "In here?"

"I think I'll float. They had to take the chains off the side doors and the back, so I'll do some laps."

"Yoshi said he'd keep an eye on the Third Street door. He's pretty much automated at this point."

"Great."

"And Kevin will be in the wings the whole time as usual."

"Okay."

"Thanks for coming tonight."

"You couldn't keep me away," he said, giving me one of those intense looks.

"How's Edgar?"

"Seems to be okay. He had a bad day, but the vet said he hadn't gotten dangerously hyperthermic. No way of knowing how long he was in there, but it couldn't have been from before yesterday evening."

"Too hot, huh." I shuddered a little, imagining being shut in a metal box in the September heat. "Thanks for that, too. I wanted to check on him last night, but with all the cops around, and all the commotion, it didn't happen."

"He's okay."

Then the showgirls came chattering down the stairs, and it was back to business. It was kind of funny; sitting out in the house, it hadn't seemed like a whole lot of people. But down in the dressing room, as they all started arriving, it was almost claustrophobic. Sid did a fade at some point, and even though one less body was technically a good thing, I wished he were still in sight.

Everyone was accounted for by seven thirty-five. Since I was down there, I led a short vocal exercise as people were getting into their first costumes. Then I put on my pink trampwear and pranced around in it, getting a wolf whistle from Victor. At ten till eight, I went up to the stage, telling everyone to follow me up as soon as they could.

At five till eight, we were all assembled onstage. I reminded everyone about the cast changes and the scene order, asked for questions, didn't get any, gave a short pep talk. And then it was "Places, please."

Kevin tapped his walkie and the overture started. From that point on I tried to stop thinking like a director, and concentrated on getting in character as the Girl. As small a part as it was, the actress in me wanted to make an impression with it if I could. I knew I couldn't pull off the clueless innocent or the ambitious idiot. So I went with Thinks She Has it Figured Out But is Getting Cold Feet. When Victor came up again for our entrance, I greeted him in character. He responded instantly with a modulation of the Ivory he'd been playing, going more overtly seductive. And man, that guy had some heat when he wanted to turn it on.

We went on and played the scene. He sang, and I couldn't help it; I started to groove a little. He went with it, taking me into a loose dance hold and singing to me. I knew it was playing differently from the night before. There was no chill tonight. He was less of a predator, but – crucially – more of a betrayer. I thought, after the fact, that I would have liked to see that scene on video.

As I sank down under the influence, Dexter caught me and swept me up for our exit. I heard some hearty applause, which was nice even though I knew most of it was for Victor. Cameron, in the holding area, was giving us a slow (silent) clap.

"Wow, where did that come from?" Victor said once we were off and safely downstairs.

"I don't know. You're too sexy for this show." He laughed. "Thanks for picking it up so fast."

"It was nice to have something to play off of." The 'for a change' was implied.

There was a flurry and scurry around us as people were getting changed for Scene 7. Victor didn't have another scene till Act II, and of course I was done. So we went back up and hung out in the makeup room, out of the way, till all the dancers had trooped up again and were in position.

I didn't see Sid anywhere, and wondered where he had gotten to.

The rest of Act I went fine, with strong applause for all the songs. And then it was intermission. By this time I'd changed back into my Director-wear (black slacks, multicolored silk tunic, and jazzy flats if you're interested), and figured I'd go back out to the house for Act II. As I left the stage and came into the seating area, I could see quite a few people in their seats with phones in hand. I hoped they were tweeting something about what a great show it was.

Everything seemed to be under control. I went up to the lobby and, after confirming there was a cop on duty, found the FOH site manager. "How'd we do on ticket sales? It looks pretty full in there."

"Box office said only thirty seats left un-filled. Ten of your backers came in tonight."

"Oh, that's great. Thanks!" That was another thing FOH was handling – the comp list. I took a pass through the mezzanine, just to get a general feel for things, and didn't overhear anybody bitching about the show. (You always hear someone bitching about the line at the ladies' room, but that is a problem no theater director can solve.)

Back in the house, I worked my way into the tech box. "Everything cool, guys?"

"We're good," said Brad. "Want me to make an announcement at the curtain call, about the re-casting?" Brad, who had what they called a face for radio, also had the voice for it and was doing all our announcements.

"Uh ... hmm. Maybe we should. Yeah, good idea." I made a note to have a correction printed for the programs for the second weekend. Then I stowed my stuff, took a drink of water, and thought if only we didn't have a killer on the loose I could relax.

Brad gave the fifteen-minute warning. I closed my eyes for a second ... and, incredibly, fell asleep.

I woke up again, disoriented and confused, as soon as the music for Cameron's second song started. Yoshi, sitting next to me, was snickering. I poked him with my elbow and took another drink of water.

Miranda's second song, a nice waltz for Liz and Felipe. Dialogue. The showgirls, at their nastiest; then

Victor and Dexter, chilling it down. I was so impressed with Dexter, hadn't really imagined that such a nice guy could create such a moral black hole with so few words. I made myself a note to record that scene for him. He might want it for his reel someday. Then it was Ivory's second song, a boogie-woogie hymn of unrepentance.

Then we were out to the street to start drawing the threads of the story together. By now I was hoping the audience was invested in Jenny and Tony, who were doing good work. Back to the Blue Note for some dialogue as the undercover operation started to wrap up. The social dancers were doing great at acting oblivious, doing their thing unobtrusively.

Yoshi's lighting design, going into the climax at the club, ensured that the dancers looked almost as if they were underwater; it threw the leads into sharp relief, without the rest of the stage being dark. Just as I was having this thought, the background music ended. The dancers separated, but 'Fox' wasn't onstage. I realized with a jolt of horror that Cameron was late.

XIV. Ysidro

I managed to be almost invisible through Act I. Hidalgo was keeping to himself, and out of everyone's way. I don't think anyone there knew the whole story except Warner and Jackson, but everyone knew he'd been busted down in the cast. No doubt there would be some chatter about it later.

For Tanith's scene as the Girl, I lurked in the left wing. I had just about recovered from the 'In the Night' number (wow, was that different from the night before) by the time Monaghan finished her first song, but I'd completely missed the showgirls doing their change to the 'I'm the One' costume. I had a feeling they were laughing at me.

Rogers did his solo, then the showgirls went on. I took the opportunity to drop down into the crypt and pass through the dressing room to the right wing. I checked out the makeup room, checked the side door, went up to the star dressing rooms; everything looked the way it should. I peered across the catwalk; it was hot as hell up there with the lights, and almost impossible to see anything with the glare. Muñoz had walked the whole thing the first time we were there. She'd bitched about it all the way back to the station, telling me it was a deathtrap, that nobody would go up there who didn't absolutely have to. Nothing looked off.

I was coming down the stairs as the showgirls went down to the dressing room; the lights were down onstage for the scene change, and the male social dancers were following the showgirls. I counted heads. There was nobody there who shouldn't have been.

The dialogue scenes went on, and the leads' song for the Act I finale. And then it was intermission.

I thought, if anything was going to happen, it would happen during intermission. So I tried to be everywhere at once. But, as we learned later, the intermission was just the access point.

Everything still seemed normal as Act II got underway. I floated some more from side to side, seeing nothing troubling. It seemed to the cast I was just part of the show at this point. Four songs, dialogue. Monaghan had gone down to the dressing room after Garcia's second song, to change for her big number. Everybody would be onstage, or in the wings, once the action moved back to the Blue Note. I started down the stairs and couldn't believe my eyes.

Redding was coming out of the crypt, holding a vodka bottle by its neck. I jumped to the floor by the men's dressing area, picking up speed, just as Monaghan saw, in her dressing mirror or peripheral vision, her danger.

Redding closed the distance fast, bringing up the bottle. Monaghan turned her head toward Redding, then away. From thirty feet away I could see the panic in her eyes.

Monaghan started up out of her chair and stumbled, lurching to the right so that Redding flew through behind her, a swing of the bottle carrying her past. Monaghan went down, rolling away as I reached Redding and grabbed her by the arm. Pulling her forward to keep her off balance, I twisted her wrist. She went with the movement and swung hard for my head.

I ducked under her arm, pulling it up behind her, and she dropped the bottle; it landed on somebody's bag with a thud. I forced Redding to the nearest wall and shoved her up against it, muttering in her ear that she was under arrest.

I got both her hands into the small of her back and pinned them there with a knee while I went for my cuffs. I was leaning on her pretty hard, and she was whimpering, but I wasn't feeling sympathetic. All this time – it seemed like a long time – I was reciting the standard cautions. Once I got the cuffs on her, I turned my head to spot Monaghan. She was on her feet, dusting herself off.

"You okay?"

"I'm okay. Shit, I'm late!" She bolted up the dressing-room stairs and I almost laughed.

I half-walked, half dragged Redding to an empty area of the men's dressing area and indicated she should lie face-down on the floor. She didn't want to, but I didn't care. Once she was down, I reached over, grabbed a necktie from somebody's station, and tied her ankles together. She started to protest.

"Make too much noise and I'll gag you, too," I promised. She shut up. I got out my phone and called Washington.

Yeah, I should have called Downtown, or maybe even 911. But I was thinking Downtown was supposed to be on this duty and they somehow let this character walk right in. In my mind, that pretty much canceled out my mistake the previous day.

Okay, she had a black wig on and didn't look much like she had the night before. But still.

Washington did the right thing, of course; once he had the information, he relayed it to our commander and then to Downtown. Their uniforms swarmed in and took Redding off my hands. They weren't too gentle with her either. Once they had her where they wanted her, I asked, "How'd you guys get in?"

"Your man in Van Nuys said someone here would open the alley door for us, that there was a show going on."

"That's right. Okay, cool." Sam must have called Jackson. "Hey, can I ask a couple questions?" I indicated that I meant to ask Redding. The uniform shrugged.

"How'd you get in here?"

"I bought a ticket," she said sullenly.

"Where'd you hide?"

"On the catwalk."

I shook my head; had to hand it to her, she'd outfoxed me. I hadn't spotted her. She had to have been all the way at the back. That none of the other almost-thirty people backstage had seen her getting upstairs, that the tech people out front hadn't seen her getting onstage, took only a bit of the sting out of it. I wouldn't say it was my worst policing since I was a rookie, but it sure hadn't been my best. The uniforms congratulated me for a good collar as they took her away. I wasn't certain I deserved it.

XV. Tanith

Valerie shot me a questioning look as the silence on stage started to stretch. I didn't know what to do. Just as I was about to tell her to drop an instrumental to fill the time while we figured something out, Cameron came on.

She looked like she'd been dodging traffic, her usual makeup embellished with smears of dust and her costume disarranged. There was a murmur from the audience. She went straight to her mark and took the mic.

Action onstage froze as the music started. Cameron's voice was a little thin, a little shaky at first. But like the pro she was, she dug into her breath and grounded herself, and fed us the song of someone who's given up, who's ready to quit, and who's found that readiness a source of strength rather than weakness ... but who is also clearly not quite in her right mind. It's a lot to convey in a short, quiet song. I applauded with the rest of the crowd when she finished.

Tony and Jenny took over then, Liz and Victor finishing the scene and the Blue Note closing for good on a blackout. The final scenes played out, Tony and Jenny did their big closing ballad, and the curtain fell.

I sat there, listening to the initial applause die down while Brad went into the casting announcement. Then the curtain call. More applause. Big applause for Victor, and a burst for Cameron. The whole cast took a bow, stepping back for the dancers to come up. Then Jenny, Tony, Victor, and Cameron came up together. Somebody in the front row stood up.

Oh, how I love theater peer pressure! Once that one person stood up, everybody else started to.

Just then, my phone buzzed. I dug it out and saw a text from Sid: *Got Redding LAPD on scene.* I may have jumped up and down in my seat a little with excitement and relief. Yoshi gave me a querying look. But I was too busy texting back to fill him in. *AWESOME you are my hero don't leave without saying goodbye.*

I leaned across Yoshi to Brad. "I'm going up to say something, okay?"

"Sure," he said, with an expression that said This is the Last Time I Do a First-Timer's Show.

The applause was diminishing, and people were starting to assemble themselves to leave as I hustled down the aisle and up the stairs. I pushed through the curtain and waved frantically to Kevin. "I need the hand mic!" He found it and turned it on for me, and I stepped back through the curtain to the front of the stage.

"Hi everybody! Drive safe home tonight, and when you get there, if you enjoyed the show, please tell all your friends. We've had a little drama offstage that may be in the news this week, but tonight's cast will be playing through next Sunday. Thanks for coming!"

Then I ducked back through the curtain, handed the mic back to Kevin with a quick "assemble in five," and went looking for Sid. I found him in the alley, where four squad cars were lined up. I could just barely see Susan, in the backseat of one of them. Seven or eight cops were standing around with their phones or their two-ways. It was quite a festive scene, actually – the cars still had their emergency lights on.

"So?" I stood close to Sid. He didn't seem to mind.

"She bought a ticket, got backstage during intermission, and hid on the catwalk ... I caught her coming out of the crypt trying to bang on Miss Monaghan with a vodka bottle."

"Good grief."

"It's going to be an interesting interrogation. Downtown's looking at all the different charges and can't quite decide where to push first."

"Well, on Billy, of course," I said acidly. "What's wrong with those guys."

One of the other cops heard me. "Detective Washington is coming in from the Valley to question the subject on the West homicide," she said. "We'll cover all the downtown incidents."

"Okay, that makes sense. Sorry," I offered. She made a dismissive gesture and turned away. "Oops," I said to Sid, who laughed.

"Don't worry about it. They're half mad because I was the one inside to bag her."

"Their commander didn't put anyone inside except in the lobby, huh. That guy's probably burning right now."

"That would be my guess." He looked like the thought amused him.

"So ... are you done for the night?"

"I sure am."

And yet, here he still was. "I have to talk to the company for a minute. Want to come in?" He nodded, and followed me in.

Kevin had the entire cast assembled onstage. I looked around the group and thought, this is a good group. This next week is going to be nothing but fun.

"How's everybody feeling? 'Cause I gotta say, I am one happy camper right now." A few people laughed, Victor started to clap, and then we all just gave ourselves a round of applause.

"You may have noticed the light show outside. Our security specialist, Detective Palacio here, has delivered your former cast-mate to the LAPD and we should now be done with all that weirdness." More applause. "You'll get the full story later, but ... for now, I'd like to take a minute to remember Billy."

Everybody hushed up fast and we had a minute of silence. Then I took a couple of deep breaths, so that my voice was only slightly shaky when I spoke again.

"Thanks. We have two shows tomorrow, so I really hope nobody is planning to go to a midnight movie, or milonga, or whatever," I said, sending a mild glare over to Felipe. He laughed and made an 'okay-okay' gesture.

"On a serious note ... I could not be more pleased with the way Jenny, Tony, Victor, and Cameron have played their parts. Red and Dexter, my heartfelt thanks for coming up to the mark so fast and so well. Miranda and Lily and Liz and Felipe ... you make this a nightclub I would want to go to. And of course Rita, Maria, Sherry, and Tasha – I think you need to see how many views the YouTube clips have already gotten. You are all fabulous."

"Marco," I went on, "you were in a difficult position this week and you did your best to be true to the show. Thank you. And last but not least, Betty and the Blue Note Dancers! You have no idea how much you all add to this production." I did a little bow and started clapping for them; the rest of the cast joined in.

"Okay, I won't keep you. Get home, get some rest, and I'll see you back here at one-thirty. Good work, everybody."

It took a while, of course, for everyone to sort themselves out and finally leave. The cast members did a good job tidying up behind themselves in the dressing room. Yoshi and Brad and Valerie logged off and locked down. Kevin double-checked all the rooms backstage. I cleaned up the makeup room (again).

Sid was waiting for me, sitting in the front row, when I came down off the stage. "I told Mr. Warner I'd walk you out," he said, standing to join me.

"Thanks," I said, pulling out my phone as it buzzed yet again. There was a text from Red. *Check your email when you get home. I got video of your scene.* "Aww!"

"What?"

"Red took a video of my scene. He must have read my mind." We were out of the theater and heading for the parking lot. When we got to my car, I looked up at him. "Thanks. For everything."

"My pleasure," said Sid. "Let me know when you want to come over and see Edgar."

"How's Monday?"

He smiled. "It just so happens I have the day off."

"Good," I said. "So do I."

XV. Ysidro

I spent most of the next day at the station, doing follow-up and paperwork, pitching in to help Sam get ready to deliver the case to the D.A. Nobody said anything about Redding hiding on the catwalk, maybe because I was at the theater on my own time anyway and if I'd chased Redding around up there and someone got hurt the department could have been in trouble. At any rate, my commander seemed to have forgiven me, but he still kept Sam on lead. I was fine with that.

Redding was, oddly, more cooperative in jail than she had been out of it. Maybe she thought she was going to get some useful career exposure out of this. She still seemed to think that she was going to *have* a career. I personally thought she'd be lucky to get a plea deal. It was the premeditation of the oxycontin that took her into straight-up homicide. We hadn't yet found the bit of history that would tell us when or where she turned into a person willing to kill. Maybe we never would.

It was tempting to call Tanith. I'd gotten used to talking to her. But I was busy, and I knew she was busy. After all, she had two shows to do. I could ping her Monday morning. Then about four-thirty, which I guessed was during the break between the shows, I got a text. *Hey Sid it's weird around here without you. Lesley said good work on bagging Susan. I told her about the vodka bottle and she said it's a shame that's in evidence*

I took a minute to write back. *Hey Tanith tell Lesley when she's unconcussed I'll send her one as an apology*

It's a deal. So how's Edgar?

Acts like nothing ever happened and he's been waiting for that pillow all his life

LOL

Want to come see him tomorrow?

Send me the address and let me know when

Now I had a dilemma. What I wanted to suggest – an afternoon meetup that might turn into dinner and possibly more - was something I could not suggest. If I suggested a time early in the day, she might think it was just a come-see-the-cat thing. That was really all it should be. Until Redding's case was resolved, Tanith was off-limits.

I didn't know if she'd thought about that. I wasn't certain she'd thought about seeing me after the case. I thought she had, but emotions are always heightened in situations like this. For all the professionalism she'd shown at the theater, I couldn't forget that she'd lost someone she cared about. That minute of silence after last night's show had been revealing.

So I took a little time composing the reply. It had to somehow say that I wanted to see her in a nonprofessional capacity and that I couldn't yet. I did not want her thinking of me as someone who would color outside the lines on something like this. And I still had some thinking of my own to do. Finally I went for 'just say it' and wrote *You are a witness so we have to keep some distance and I regret that. How about a quick visit around noon.* I entered the address and sent it off.

A few minutes later I got a reply that told me she was going to handle this professionally too. *Understood, Lesley loves cats and we can't have one so can I bring her? She's been asked to come by the station tomorrow so I was heading your way anyhow*

That works. See you tomorrow, have a good show tonight

Tsk tsk Detective, it's 'break a leg'

Seems like a sick thing to say to somebody

You have a point. That was the end of the exchange. The next day, both of them came by. Edgar was his usual mellow self, Tanith and Lesley badgered me about the case, I tried not to tell them anything I shouldn't, and then they headed back out again so Lesley could go over her statement with Sam. She went out first. Tanith hung back for a minute. She stared at me for a second, then said, "So until she's sentenced, right?"

"Right. Or until there's a plea bargain."

"That is annoying." Her gaze was on my mouth.

I laughed, I couldn't help it. There was definitely something about her expression that said 'the rules are stupid.' With her standing close to me, I tended to agree with her. "Probably six months or so if she goes to trial."

"Jeez, really? If she pleads out, how long?"

"Could be a couple of months."

"That is better."

"I agree," I said. There was a long silent minute in which neither of us moved. Then I shook my head a little, took a step back, and said, "I'll text you a picture of Edgar from time to time. Let you know how he's doing."

"Okay," she said after a moment. "Be careful out there."

"I will." Oh, how I wanted to reach across the space between us. Instead I watched her turn around and go.

187

We got lucky. Susan Redding's public defender offered a plea, and the prosecutor made the deal because he didn't trust that a jury would convict this harmless-looking young woman. By then I'd sent approximately (okay, exactly) a dozen texts with pictures of Edgar, and received a dozen replies. None of those had pictures, and none of them said anything that would put either of us in the wrong, but all of them let me know that Tanith was counting down the days, same as I was. When I found out about the plea deal, a week after the fact and two months after Tanith's show closed, Redding had already been shipped out.

So that week, instead of another picture of my cat, I sent a link to the court notice. About a half hour later, I got a voice call from Tanith. "Does this mean I can ask you out now?"

"I think it does."

"Well, let's be really sure about this, because I don't want to go to jail for dating a cop. That seems ridiculously ironic."

I almost laughed. She could probably tell. "You won't go to jail. But I could handcuff you if you like."

"Detective Palacio, what an outrageous suggestion. You must not be at the station. I was thinking more along the lines of some salsa dancing."

"I am not at the station, so I'll say salsa dancing would be great. When and where?"

"Will we run into any of your cop buddies at the Mayan?"

"If we do, I won't let them arrest you. How's Friday?"

"Friday works. You know where to find me."

That I did. Now all I had to do was hope a new case didn't blow up on me.

XVI. Tanith

Was that a long two months? Halloween, my birthday, Thanksgiving, and all I had to show for it was a dozen pictures of this goofy alley cat. Here we were in December and finally I was putting that hot-pink dress on again.

Lesley was leaning on the frame of the bathroom door, watching me do my makeup. "You know, I didn't pick up on it at the theater," she said. "With everything going on. If I hadn't known you all these years I might not have picked up on it when we went to see the cat. And then he came to closing night. You still played it pretty cool."

"He could have gotten in big trouble."

"Stupid rules."

"Yeah. Every rule is stupid when you want to break it."

She laughed. "He is cute."

"Yes he is." I turned around so she could assess my handiwork. "About right for the Mayan?"

"Like I would know?" She looked me over critically. "Well, I'd bang you."

It was my turn to laugh. I'd gained back a little of the weight I'd lost during the last push of the play, and the dress looked even better now. I mean, 'better' in the sense of tramptastic. I knew Sid would remember it. Just the thought of his hand on my bare back had me feeling a little warm. I turned back to the mirror, confirmed that now was the time to stop with the makeup, confirmed that my hair was doing what I wanted it to do. It was a little shorter now and I was wearing it loose. "Not bad for thirty-six."

"You still look twenty-two. When is he getting here?"

"Any minute." She stood back and let me exit the bathroom, going barefoot down the hall to my room to collect my club-going cross-body evening bag, my shoes, and a coat. The last item was something Lesley had made for me about a month ago, when I had – in a moment of wine-induced weakness – revealed the double motivation for buying the pink dress and the shoes. The coat was cut like a knee-length duster, made out of black denim, and decorated on the back with a collage of appliqué flowers in crimson, hot pink, and orange, all beaded and rhinestoned and fabulous. Best of all, it had pockets. "Thanks for this," I said, because now Lesley was standing in my bedroom doorway. "It's perfect."

"I know." We heard the doorbell. "It seems we have company. Is Red answering the door?"

We both stood still and listened. Sure enough, we heard the door open, heard Red greet Sid, and then the door closed again. "Time to make my entrance," I said. I was feeling a little nervous. Lesley took the coat, because – as she'd told me – I needed to go out there in just the dress. I slung on the little evening bag and went out to the living room. My heels were going tap-tap on the floor. Both men were looking at me as I came around the corner from the hall.

"If I'd known you were wearing that, I would've put 'In the Night' on." Red had his eyebrows up.

Sid's reaction was also highly satisfactory. He was smiling a little, with his lips parted as if he'd started to say something and then forgotten what it was, and his gaze was warm. He was wearing a black knit shirt and jeans under a gray velvet blazer. It looked as soft as mouse fur. "What did Edgar think of that jacket?" I said.

"He tried to sit on it. Ready to go wow the crowd?" He held out a hand. I turned toward Lesley and she helped me into the coat. I can't remember if I said anything else to her or Red. Sid looked so good, and being in the same room with him again was all I needed to confirm that yes, this was worth waiting for.

I took Sid's hand and we went outside, he opened the car door for me and watched as I drew my legs inside. When he got into the driver's seat and closed his door, he didn't start the car right away. Instead he looked over at me and said, "This was worth waiting for," and leaned toward me.

I closed the distance and kissed him. It felt like coming home. After a minute I said, "Thank all the gods we didn't have to wait six months."

"For real," he said, and we both laughed. Then he started the car.

I was kind of expecting him to know what he was doing on the dance floor, and he did. I hadn't been out dancing for a really long time, and I was really enjoying it, but the band never played a slow song and by eleven I was ready for something else. Sid must have been reading my mind because he said, "These guys don't know how to play a rumba."

"Well," I said, pretending to consider it, "there's no law that says we have to dance as fast as the music."

He studied my face for a moment while he listened. "Challenge accepted." He put his hand on my back again – oh mercy, I thought – and brought me in close. I slid my left hand up his shoulder. He'd checked that soft gray jacket. I could feel the solid muscle under the thin fabric of his shirt. I moved my hand just a bit more so I could touch the hair brushing his collar. He took my right hand in his left and started dancing again.

I think he did a good job, but to be honest after a minute or so all I could really pay attention to was his hand, now all the way around my back, and his cologne, just a breath of it, and his body close to mine. I closed my eyes and turned my head a few degrees so that my face was against his. "I'm glad you're not super tall," I said softly.

"Me too." He loosened his hold just a little bit. I tipped my head back and he kissed me.

XVI. Ysidro

That first kiss in the car was one thing. The kiss on the dance floor was leveling up in a big way. When her mouth opened under mine I thought was going to pass out. She tasted like the maraschino cherry from her cocktail, and she made a soft sound, and her hand went into my hair. I didn't want to open my eyes, but I had to get us off the dance floor. We moved a few feet and I kissed her again. "Do you mind if we go now?" I said, a bit breathlessly.

"I was hoping you would say that. Can you take me to see Edgar?"

"If I do, you won't get home till tomorrow morning." It was only fair to warn her.

"Good." She took her hands off me, looked around, and walked across the bar to the restroom. That seemed prudent, so I went that way too. We didn't say much to each other as we went to the coat check, as we waited for the valet, and as I maneuvered us out of downtown. Once I hit a clear lane on the freeway, she said, "I can't believe I've only known you for a week."

That was about what it amounted to. Two months of texts did not equal two months of dating. "Well, it was kind of an extraordinary week," I said after a minute.

"I've never been with someone who wasn't in the industry somehow. Actor, writer, musician, whatever." I didn't know what to say to that. She added, "You figured out Red and I had a thing. Lesley probably gave us up." I huffed out a laugh. "It was back in college. We're honestly just good friends now."

"I know." After a minute I said, "It's not easy being with a cop. Sometimes the hours are really bad, there'll be missed calls and missed dates, and stuff that just doesn't get done. And the work can be dangerous."

"What's the worst you've ever dealt with?"

"Drug den. Lots of lead flying. It was the kind of shootout you see on a TV show and think, does that shit really happen? It does. One of my team got hit in the leg, he was in the hospital for a week and then off duty for two months."

"Well, Red almost got killed on a set once. Prop failure. Kind of like the thing with the play, only it wasn't sabotage, something just broke. If he didn't have good reflexes and wasn't super strong, he would have fallen forty feet."

"Shit happens. All you can do is be as prepared as possible." We were getting close to my place now. "You sure you want to do this?" I could tell she was staring at me.

"I'd never forgive myself if I didn't at least try," she said eventually. "I've never known anybody like you."

"Same goes." I parked my car. "You're so damn smart."

"But you're not threatened by me. You know who you are. You're good at what you do. Everything else I really needed to know has kind of been answered tonight."

"Everything?" I smiled at her.

"You can learn a lot about a person from a dance. Or a kiss."

"That is true." I leaned over to kiss her again. That might have been a mistake. When I finally sat back I was not in a fit state to walk to my condo. I put my head back and tried to steady my breath. "We could actually get arrested for that."

"Seriously? Arrested?" She didn't believe me. "Oh." She tugged her skirt down, laughing under her breath. "Maybe we should go inside, then."

"Don't move," I said. She stayed obediently in her seat while I got out of the car and went around to open her door. She put her hand in mine and swung those gorgeous legs out, shifting her weight forward to stand up. I put my arm around her, closed the car door with my other hand, pressed the lock button on the key, and started for home.

When we got upstairs and went inside, she went looking for Edgar first thing. "Hey Mr. Cat, did you miss me?" He stared at her suspiciously, like he'd never seen her before. "Ungrateful little bastard," she said. "Who brought you kibble at the theater?" He still looked unimpressed. She looked over at me. "I guess rescuing him from a dumpster makes you the hero."

"Well, yeah," I said. "You want some coffee?"

She walked back to me, shedding the coat and draping it over the back of a chair. "Not right now." She moved in on me, brushing her hands up my lapels, then slid her hands underneath and pushed the jacket off my shoulders and down my arms. She caught it and threw it on a chair, then set her hands on my chest. I put my hands on her bare sides, thumbs running underneath the front of the dress, along the bottom of her rib cage. She dug one hand into my hair and brought my mouth down to hers.

I lost track of time for a while. When we came up for air, I was leaning on the kitchen wall and Tanith was right up against me, her skirt gathered in one of my hands. The other one was on her ass, which was next-best-thing to bare. "You know, the first time I saw this dress, I thought it was not quite up to code," I said. She laughed, forehead pressed to my shoulder. I moved my hand, fingers sliding under the g-string again, up to the front and then around back. She sucked in a breath. "What do you want to do?"

"I want to get out of these shoes. And everything else, basically." My shirt was already untucked. She pushed it up and started pulling it over my head. I helped. "Jesus, Sid. What kind of workout do you do?"

"Is that really what you most want to know right now?"

She laughed again. "I'm nervous. I haven't done this for a while."

"You're nervous? The woman who can get thirty grown-ass adults to do anything she wants?"

"Well, when you put it that way." She kissed me again, hands on my bare chest, and I almost forgot I even had a bedroom. When she went for my belt I remembered.

"One of us is going to fall over," I said. "I'd rather we got horizontal in an intentional manner." I already had an arm around her waist, so I started walking, pretty sure she'd come with me. I steered us through the dark living/dining room and down the short hall. She sat down on the bed and started unbuckling a shoe. I knelt down to get the other one. I didn't get up, just took my pants off right there and waited for the next signal.

"I've got you right where I want you, Detective," she said, and dropped the g-string on the floor. She must have wriggled out of it while I was getting undressed. I ran my hands up her legs, pushing up that little scrap of a skirt, and breathed her in. "Jesus!"

"What do I need to know, before I'm not in a state to remember it."

"IUD. Clean at latest checkup. I want you."

"I did need to know that," I said, and put my mouth on her.

XVII. Tanith

Somewhere in the middle of the night, he told me about his workout (kettlebells, boxing, capoeira) and I told him about mine. That was after I did a thing he wasn't expecting, a thing that took some strength. After he got done laughing, I told him how I'd asked Red for some weapons training so I could go out for a part as a warrior elf in a fantasy movie.

"Did you get the part?" I was lying with my head on his shoulder. His voice was soft, like the dusting of hair around his navel. He was ticklish there. Everything else seemed to be erogenous. Of course, I kind of felt the same way, and it might have been a function of our ten-plus-weeks of wanting this, but I wouldn't have sworn to that.

After a moment I remembered the question. "Um. Yeah. I got to use a broadsword. The fight coordinator couldn't believe it when I used a standard-weight weapon. It was only a few days of filming, but it got me some other things."

"I guess you're always having to learn new stuff."

"Same as you. I distracted you, didn't I." Could not have kept the smug tone out of my voice for any money.

"On the Million Dollar case? Yeah, you did. You weren't trying to."

"I'm glad you didn't go running around the catwalk that night. That bitch probably would have pushed you off, the show would've been fucked beyond recovery, and we wouldn't be here."

He laughed again. "I didn't want to believe anyone would willingly go out there. You have to admit, it was a good hiding place."

"Yeah, if you're willing to risk setting your hair on fire. Out there when the lights are off is one thing. With the lights on, that's just bonkers." I took a second. "Of course, considering the subject, yeah, you should have looked out there." He smacked my ass lightly. "So what are we going to do?"

He didn't ask what I meant. "I hope we're going to do a lot of this. Do you like going on dates?"

"I'm trying to remember." He laughed under his breath. "Yes, of course, I like going out to movies or dinner or dancing once in a while. But I also like staying home with a book and a DVD and some takeout. I'm always going to be working side gigs. Writing or producing or acting, whatever I can get."

"So what you're saying is you're going to be as hard to pin down as I will."

"Probably, yeah. Most of my vacation time goes to outside projects. And a lot of my weekends." The last time I'd had a planning-a-relationship conversation it had degenerated quickly, because the guy wanted to set all the terms. I was hoping pretty hard that Sid would be more of a grown-up.

"Do you like to be chased?"

Eeek. "Uh, no. Not per se. I don't do this stuff to be hard to get. I do it because I have to, to keep my sanity."

"Okay," he said after a moment. "Well, we don't live too far apart. Both our jobs are based in the Valley. If one or the other of us has a free night, are you okay with short-notice invitations?"

"Yeah, sure. If you got off shift at six or seven, wanted to get together for dinner or whatever, you could call."

"Same on this side. So let's try that for a while. Because I'd love to be able to say, oh yeah, every Friday night for sure. But that's a hopeless goal. I couldn't even promise every Sunday morning."

I hitched myself up so I could look in his eyes. "You don't have to promise anything. I don't expect dancing every time. I don't expect great sex every time."

"Was it great?" he said, looking interested. "I mean, I thought so."

I rolled my eyes. "Yeah, Sid, it was great. You are different." I let that sink in. "You are in a class of your own. I don't have comparable experience. So I can't begin to guess how this will go. I just know I want to try."

"Okay." He pulled me down for a kiss. "Same on this side. We'll play it by ear." He considered that for a second. "What does that actually mean? I never thought about it before."

"That means like if you're a piano player and you hear a song, you can play it just by hearing it. You don't need the sheet music."

"So that is not the right metaphor for this situation." I laughed, I couldn't help it. He was smiling up at me. "But I could say I want you to be my leading lady for the foreseeable future. Can you work with that?"

"Yeah," I said. "I can work with that."

THE END

If you enjoyed MILLION DOLLAR DEATH, please consider leaving a positive rating or review. It really helps self-published authors find an audience! Thanks for reading.

Want more? Bonus material ahead!

AN ACTING LESSON

Tanith: Okay Marco. What are we shooting for here?

Marco: I'm not sure I still want to be an actor.

Tanith: Why not? Because of one bad experience?

Marco: I feel like maybe I don't belong here.

Tanith: You think you're not good enough?

Marco: Kind of.

Tanith: There's this exercise maybe we should do.

Marco: What is it?

Tanith: Pull your chair over to face me. Closer.
Okay, good.

Marco: Now what?

Tanith: I'm going to say something and you give me
one line back. Not as a character, as you. Tell me
who you are.

Marco: Huh?

Tanith: Tell me who you are.

Marco: Uh, I'm Marco and I'm from El Paso ... .

Tanith: Not your vital statistics. Tell me who you are.

Marco: I played football in high school.

Tanith: Not what you did. Tell me who you are.

Marco: My grandmother set up my first date.

Tanith: Not about your family. Tell me who you are.

Marco: I'm shy.

Tanith: That's better. Tell me who you are.

Marco: I feel like I scare people.

Tanith: Tell me who you are.

Marco: I'm a good driver.

Tanith: Tell me who you are.

Marco: I'm scared of auditions.

Tanith: Tell me who you are.

Marco: I feel ridiculous when I dance.

Tanith: Tell me who you are.

Marco: I was a virgin until I was nineteen.

Tanith: Tell me who you are.

Marco: I'm ... kind of angry sometimes.

Tanith: Tell me who you are.

Marco: Being angry scares me.

Tanith: Tell me who you are.

Marco: I resent not getting my family's support for what I want to do.

Tanith: Okay, good. We'll come back to that. Have you ever seen a counselor, or done therapy?

Marco: No.

Tanith: I kind of figured. What's this about your family?

Marco: Nobody thinks I'm going to make it. Everybody's always "so when you coming home?"

Tanith: What do you tell them?

Marco: Last time I said "why should I come home?"

Tanith: What did they say?

Marco: They said "if you're just going to work at Best Buy you could do that here."

Tanith: Bitches!

Marco: (laughing) Yeah.

Tanith: Now tell me the last five things you auditioned for.

Marco: Your show, a TV cop show, a cop movie, a stoner movie, a TV sitcom.

Tanith: And what were the last five jobs you got?

Marco: Your show, the cop movie – the one where I met Mr. West - the stoner movie, and before that two gigs as an extra.

Tanith: So you actually got hired for three out of five of the last speaking roles you read for.

Marco: Huh. I guess I did.

Tanith: Why did you choose those particular projects?

Marco: I thought I could handle them.

Tanith: Did you come out to L.A. wanting to be a star?

Marco: Well sure, doesn't everybody?

Tanith: When you think of "movie star" who do you think of?

Marco: Like, Tom Cruise.

Tanith: What do you think of critics who say Tom Cruise always plays himself?

Marco: Uh ... I guess I don't care. He's always good.

Tanith: Here's what I think. I think most of the biggest movie stars back to the beginning of movies always play themselves. Charlie Chaplin was always Charlie Chaplin. Humphrey Bogart was always Humphrey Bogart. And Tom Cruise is always Tom Cruise. What makes them stars is the ability to be themselves in a fantastic situation. Know what I mean?

Marco: I'm not sure.

Tanith: You're looking at an actor who is consistently successful in a certain genre, but the roles really are different people. Different characters. The script as written does not say Harrison Ford, or whoever, it says Indiana Jones. Indiana Jones is not Han Solo is not Jack Ryan.

Marco: Like ... say it's Tom Cruise, maybe he approaches it like, okay, this is my situation and my back story and these are my character's distinguishing features. Now what do I do, as this character, in this situation.

Tanith: That's what I think. I don't think he goes in with this whole Method thing of "I have to live like a vampire, I have to become a vampire, in order to play Lestat."

Marco: He was good in that movie.

Tanith: Personally, I think he was better than Brad Pitt, by miles, in that movie. Brad is great in some things. Not that.

Marco: So what you're saying is if I want to be a movie star I need to figure out myself and how I would behave in different situations.

Tanith: Right, exactly. A lot of actors do some talk therapy to access their emotional responses in a safe place.

Marco: Where I come from, nobody even talks about getting therapy.

Tanith: Yeah well. Texas.

(Laughter)

Tanith: And it helps to know a little bit about the context you'll be playing in. A director or writer may not give you a whole pile of context. But that's what the Internet is for. Playing Lestat? Look up New Orleans in the early 19th century. What was the standard of behavior. Any clues about body language. How did they wear their clothes.

Marco: (making notes) This is great.

Tanith: Okay. Ever read for any of the historical or fantasy things that are so big now?

Marco: No.

Tanith: Why not?

Marco: Well, I don't know anything about that stuff.

Tanith: Let me tell you the first big secret of making a living as an actor.

Marco: What's that?

Tanith: You have to audition for Every Fucking Thing.

Marco: (laughing) But I can't do accents or whatever. Except Spanish.

Tanith: Get an English accent, and maybe Middle Eastern, and you're okay. You have a full-time job, right?

Marco: Uh ... yeah.

Tanith: Where does all your money go?

Marco: Uh ... I don't know.

Tanith: I suggest you make a budget. I can direct you to a couple of good websites. You will start tracking your spending and find out where your money goes, and you will stop wasting it – I guarantee you will find some places where you are wasting it – and you will start investing in yourself. Know any martial arts?

Marco: No.

Tanith: Marco, really now. You're a big, strong guy with a sports background. You've got a multi-ethnic sort of look. You should be cleaning up in the action parts.

Marco: My first movie part was a football movie.

Tanith: Which is great, but there are only so many football movies. You want to be equipped to play in any kind of sports movie. You don't have to be an expert. You just need to know the basic moves, the rules, the language, and how to handle the gear.

Marco: My teachers never talked about that. It was all, you know, Shakespeare and Ibsen and, and Scorsese.

Tanith: Study that stuff too, but how many movies get made based on Ibsen plays?

Marco: Uh ... .

Tanith: Exactly. See, this action stuff, even I've been hired for, because Red taught me enough to read for a fantasy thing where I needed to handle a sword. There's so much of this stuff.

Marco: I guess.

Tanith: I mean, how good an actor is Liam Neeson?

Marco: He's phenomenal.

Tanith: But he's a star because of action movies. Not because of "Michael Collins."

Marco: Never saw that.

Tanith: My point. Look. You have the power to limit yourself, but you also have the power to expand your range. Study on YouTube. Take a class here and there. If there's any place to learn any of these arts, it's Los Angeles.

Marco: I'm feeling like an idiot now.

Tanith: Did you think once you graduated from college, you were done?

Marco: I guess I did.

Tanith: But wasn't that boring? Were you really excited about having a career playing extras on cop shows?

Marco: I wasn't. You're right. I was boxing myself in just because I wasn't thinking I should keep learning.

Tanith: Learning new stuff is fun. You meet new people, you make connections, but mostly your brain just has a party because New Shiny Stuff!

(Laughter)

Tanith: Tell me who you are.

Marco: I'm an actor.

THE END

DRAMATIS PERSONAE: WHAT WENT DOWN

As envisioned for "MILLION DOLLAR DEATH," these parts are originally played by the (fictional) actors, singers, and dancers named.

CASSANDRA – a professional woman, mid to late thirties; Jenny Wilson
EVAN – a bartender/undercover cop, mid to late thirties; Tony Rogers
IVORY – club owner/manager and general scumbag; Victor Garcia
FOX – a young singer/songwriter; Cameron Monaghan
SAMMY – a dance hostess/bartender; Liz Loving
LARRY – a dance host; Felipe Matamoros
CRYSTAL – a stripper; Lily Chen
SINGER; Miranda Parker
GIRL; Susan Redding
HENCHMAN; Marco Hidalgo
MICKEY – a plainclothes detective; Billy West
WAITER 1; Billy West
WAITER 2; Dexter Parker
BLACK BOX GIRLS (LACEY, STACEY, PIXIE, AND TRIXIE); Rita Gonzalez, Maria Pocatello, Sherry Toyama, and Tasha Jefferson
BLUE NOTE DANCERS; Mark, Jaime, Phil, Jerry, Anthony, Marilyn, Laura, and Sheila
PROMPT/RUNNER – Betty

The (fictional) technical crew for the production of WHAT WENT DOWN as described in MILLION DOLLAR DEATH are:

Tanith Salazar – writer/producer/director
Kevin Jackson – stage manager
Drew "Red" Warner – prop master/sets
Lesley Hayes – wardrobe mistress
Yoshi Ito – lighting and projections
Brad Stockton – sound
Valerie Benton – composer, producer

LIST OF MUSICAL NUMBERS

Act I:
Dance With Me – Singer
When I'm Not With You – Black Box Girls
In the Night – Ivory
One Time – Fox
Suspicion/Undercover Tango – Evan
I'm the One – Black Box Girls
When I See You Again – Evan and Cassandra

Act II:
Without You – Fox
If I Wanted Love – Singer
One Track Mind – Black Box Girls
Speak No Evil – Ivory
The Way to Die – Fox
Alley Cat – Black Box Girls
Never Alone – Evan and Cassandra

The full script of WHAT WENT DOWN follows.

WHAT WENT DOWN was an experiment. A series of books (the Burke novels by Andrew Vachss) inspired a short story treatment, which in turn inspired a song. Before I knew it, I had a whole play.

But what does a person do with a play? Well, in my case, nothing much. Until I started writing contemporary fiction, and then I thought *maybe there is a story that could wrap around that play*. That story became the short novel MILLION DOLLAR DEATH, which you may have just read. Incidentally, the Million Dollar Theater is a real thing in downtown Los Angeles.

A few notes about WHAT WENT DOWN:

First, all of the song lyrics included are original. All rights are reserved. It may be that you "hear" these songs to your own music, but please don't record or perform them without permission. Find me via www.thelastories.com.

Second, the music for the songs hasn't yet been notated. That will only be done if someone says "hey I want to produce this play." Or, you know, if somebody options MILLION DOLLAR DEATH and wants the original music.

Third, the scene numbering tracks with the production as described in MILLION DOLLAR DEATH.

Fourth, the action in the play takes place in the 1980s, in a large city not unlike New York. It is about a woman searching for a girl, and a good man trying to pin down a bad man, and how they intersect. It is, in its way, and like everything else I've written, a love story.

WHAT WENT DOWN

Overture: "Suspicion"

Curtain up on black stage. As music fades, projection fades in on upstage scrim: a skyline view, twilight. Pull downstage scrim to reveal

Act I

Prologue. *Int* an office records room. Onstage are CASSANDRA, a professional woman, and MICKEY, a professional man. Both are seated at a rectangular table under unflattering fluorescent lights; metal filing cabinets line the walls. Back flat includes "window" with closed miniblinds. *(Note: this set can be placed at center, downstage, with Scene 1 set concealed behind side curtains and upstage scrim.)*

CASSANDRA: Look, I really appreciate your help with this.

MICKEY: Well, just tell me what you want.

CASSANDRA: We represent a company that owns some property downtown. A name has come up in connection with the property that has also come up in connection with some personal business of mine

MICKEY: How personal?

CASSANDRA: About as personal as it gets. I've recently made contact with the couple who adopted my daughter, a long time ago. Under ordinary circumstances I think they might not have been glad to hear from me, but as it happens, the girl has disappeared. I would have pursued it anyway, but they begged me to help.

MICKEY: Have they contacted the police?

CASSANDRA: They filed a missing-persons report, but the girl is almost eighteen and had finished her first year of college ... not much has been done with it.

MICKEY: Early admission? (making a note)

CASSANDRA: Yeah, she's bright. But it looks like she got in with a wrong crowd.

MICKEY: It happens. So, what's your question for me?

CASSANDRA: My question is, can you tell me if the department is working on this person at this business. (slides a card across the table)

MICKEY: You think this person is involved?

CASSANDRA: I got the name from some college friends of hers.

MICKEY: I'll see what I can do.

Lights down. Drop downstage scrim for set change. Projection – nighttime traffic. Music: If I Wanted Love (instr). Pull downstage scrim to reveal

Scene 1: Int. The Blue Note, a dance hall & bar. Onstage are EVAN, a bartender; various, mostly male, customers; a young, female SINGER; dance hosts, SAMMY (a girl) and LARRY (a guy). The bar at stage left is lit with LED. The dance floor is lit with black light and flanked on the right by a cluster of club chairs with side tables. Hosts wear white. Blue neon sign: The Blue Note, above centered platform upstage. Cue music:

Song: Dance with Me *(Foxtrot:* LARRY *and SAMMY featured)*

SINGER

When I'm with you
walking in the moonlight, hand in hand
writing little love notes in the sand
that wash away at break of day
It's so romantic
walking close and kissing by the sea
Only one thing missing that we need so,
come on and dance with me
Once I saw you
no one else could ever do for me
no one else could ever make me feel the way you do,
it's something to
remember always
a once in a lifetime love affair
paradise is waiting, take me there just
come on and dance with me
It really isn't such a mystery
that I'm so happy when you dance with me
all I need is you and to be in your arms
it's really alarming that you're so charming
Since I found you
Everything is falling into place
Ever since I saw your smiling face
and big bright eyes, I'm hypnotized
by all the changes
ever since you waltzed right through my door
one thing always makes me love you more
so come on and dance with me, the music's playing
come on and dance with me.

Exit SINGER, upstage right. LARRY and SAMMY separate and find other partners as instrumental reprise of opening song plays under following action.

Scene 2. *Int.* Enter CASSANDRA, stage right. She takes in the scene, makes her way across the dance floor to the bar, hitches herself up on a stool.

EVAN: What can I get you?

CASSANDRA: A Cosmopolitan.

EVAN: Of course. (turns away and mixes the drink)

CASSANDRA: I know, it's cheesy.

EVAN: Hey, just because a lot of people like it doesn't make it bad. (hands her the drink)

> CASSANDRA turns away to watch the dancers, sipping her drink.

CASSANDRA: Popular place?

EVAN: We do all right. Haven't seen you here before.

CASSANDRA: Thought I'd try something different.

EVAN: Do you dance?

CASSANDRA: I've been known to.

EVAN: How'd you hear about us?

CASSANDRA: Someone in my office .

> CASSANDRA finishes her drink. EVAN tops it up with the remnants in the shaker.

CASSANDRA: Why, thank you. (flashes a smile)

EVAN: Just whistle when you're ready for round two.

215

CASSANDRA: Whistle, huh?

EVAN: Sure. (smiles) You know how to whistle, don't you?

CASSANDRA: Just put my lips together and blow.

> EVAN turns away to serve other customers, still smiling.

Lights down briefly.

Scene *(cont.)* Int The Blue Note. Same night; some time has passed. Instr., "If I wanted love" is playing. CASSANDRA remains at the bar.

EVAN: It's almost showtime and you haven't danced once.

CASSANDRA: Is that an invitation?

EVAN: I believe it is.

> EVAN comes around the bar, offers his arm. They dance a slow waltz. Lights change as music ends. Blue neon sign goes off, bar lights go down, black light goes off, platform lighting comes on. Dance hosts exit.

EVAN: Going to stay for the show?

CASSANDRA: What's the show?

EVAN: This is a whole 'nother place after eleven.

CASSANDRA: You don't say.

EVAN: I've gotta get back to the bar. Make yourself comfortable.

Scene 3. CASSANDRA takes a barstool upstage as a red neon light: The Black Box flickers on above the platform. Scattered customers applaud. Women CUSTOMERS exit, stage right. A HENCHMAN enters from backstage left. Burlesque chorus girls in cute, skimpy costumes file onto stage as we cue music:

Song - When I'm Not With You *(swing)*

BLACK BOX GIRLS

I can run around or I can play the game
I can work it honey till I go insane
But I can't help feeling that it's not the same
When I'm not with you!
(Let me tell you)
I can stay out late and I can dance all night
come home singing in the morning light
but all the same somehow it's just not right
when I'm not with you!
I want to
see your face in the morning sleepy
make you laugh or make you sigh impatiently
hang around till you know I'm greedy
for all the time with you that I can get
I want to
wake you up with some lovin' kissing
tell you secrets that I know you'll listen to
make my friends see what they've been missing
when they see how in love a girl can get
and you'll see
when I've got you back with me I won't let go
I pray you'll want to stay because I love you so
you can't imagine now but pretty soon you'll know
that it's fated, slated, meant to be -
one day I will be with you!

CASSANDRA laughs and applauds along with the men. EVAN watches her. Black Box Girls exit and Stripper (CRYSTAL) enters.

Scene 4. CRYSTAL begins a striptease act to instr. "Alley Cat." The HENCHMAN looks intimidating at the side of the stage. CASSANDRA turns to EVAN.

CASSANDRA: I see what you mean about a whole 'nother place.

EVAN: A little class, a little sass, the boss says.

CASSANDRA: No kidding. You work here long?

EVAN: Not too long. It's a fun gig. (glances at stripper)

CASSANDRA: Do tell.

EVAN: So where do you work?

CASSANDRA: At a law firm, in midtown.

EVAN: This is a little out of your way, isn't it?

CASSANDRA: Actually I don't live far from here. That's why I decided to try it.

EVAN: Nothing like a short commute.

CASSANDRA: Oh yeah? What neighborhood?

EVAN: Upstairs.

CASSANDRA: (laughing) How convenient!

     CRYSTAL finishes her act (down to g-string and pasties) and walks over to the bar.

CRYSTAL: Light me up, honey.

EVAN: You got it, Crystal.

> EVAN pours a glass of whisky, pulls a pack of cigarettes from under the bar, gives CRYSTAL a cig and lights it for her, then goes to serve another customer. Action behind throughout: social dancers.

CRYSTAL: Thanks, sugar. (Looks at CASSANDRA) You like the show?

CASSANDRA: I thought it was great. Are you here every night?

CRYSTAL: No, just a few weeknights. Weekends I have a gig uptown.

CASSANDRA: Well, you were really good. (lifts her drink in a mock toast. Glances at the lit cigarette) You know, those things can kill you.

CRYSTAL: Lots of things could kill me. I like to smoke.

CASSANDRA: (brief pause) I like steak and ice cream, myself.

> The women smile at each other. EVAN comes back up the bar.

EVAN: So can I get anything else for you ladies?

CASSANDRA: No thanks, I think I'm done for tonight. What's my tab?

EVAN: (hands her a slip) Hope we see you back here soon.

CASSANDRA: You never know. (hands over a few bills)

CRYSTAL: Next time, I'll get you a dance with Larry.

CASSANDRA: The guy with the Mr. T chains?

CRYSTAL: Yeeaaaah.

> They grin; exit CASSANDRA. EVAN watches her go.

CRYSTAL: She was nice.

EVAN: Yeah, she was. She was.

Lights down.

A voice in the darkness:

EVAN: Somebody gives you something, maybe one day it's free, but eventually there's a price. Be sure it's one you can pay.

Scene 5. *Int,* The Black Box, after closing. Neon and platform lights are off, customers are gone. EVAN is standing partially concealed by the drapes downstage left. Enter IVORY, upstage, with a young, nervous-looking GIRL; HENCHMAN follows them in but hangs back. EVAN backs up further into the shadows.

GIRL: What would I have to do?

IVORY: Nothing bad. This is about opening doors, baby.

GIRL: Maybe my idea of bad is different from yours.

IVORY: Well, nobody's keeping you here.

> IVORY looks at his watch, like ho-hum, boring girl.

GIRL: Can this really get me noticed?

IVORY: You better believe it, baby. Here, this will help you relax.

> IVORY gives the GIRL a pill; the HENCHMAN crosses to the bar for a glass of water. The GIRL takes the water and swallows the pill.

Enter the Black Box Girls, in various stages of undress. They don't look so cute anymore. Cue music:

Song - In the Night *(doo-wop in 6/8 time: backup by Black Box Girls)*

IVORY

In the dark, in the night
looking for someone, looking for light
now you know you're with me, you're safe as can be
in the night
(oh in the night, don't look back at the light)
in the dark, in the night
you can't see me holding you tight
But you know you're with me, you'll never be free
in the night
(oh in the night, in the night)
why would you want to go?
What do you want to know?
What would you tell me, If you could?
Everything you might need
Oh I'm a friend indeed
I'll give you something to make you feel good
(make you feel good!)
In the dark, in the night
now that I've found you, found my light
come with me, here's the way,
there's no need to pay until the night

GIRL: I'm feeling better now.

IVORY: So? Right down these stairs, baby. I'll take good care of you.

GIRL: Okay.

IVORY: That's my girl.

> IVORY and the GIRL start off, right. The GIRL starts to sag against him; he holds her up. EVAN moves forward, out of concealment but the others have their backs to him. The HENCHMAN steps forward and lifts her off her feet. Exit all but EVAN.

EVAN: And another one bites the dust. God damn it.

> EVAN throws his towel on the bar. Exit EVAN, stage left.

Lights down. Double scrim for set change. Projection on upstage scrim: a skyline view, nighttime. Music: In the Night reprise. Pull downstage scrim to reveal

Scene 6. *Int*, an office storeroom as in the prologue, distinguished by tattered posters indicating a police station. (Note: same pieces are used. Reversible back flat. Turn file cabinets face-on for prologue, side for S.6) Enter EVAN through door upstage, followed by MICKEY.

EVAN: Thanks for coming down to the precinct.

MICKEY: I'm off tonight, was kind of at loose ends. Whaddaya got?

EVAN: I got a big mess, is what I got. I've been under at this job for about two months. At first they just had me working the early shift - the Blue Note - but about two weeks ago they put me on for the burlesque show.

MICKEY: And where's the problem?

EVAN: The problem is downstairs. Every so often - twice since I've been there - the head guy brings in a girl and they go downstairs.

MICKEY: And then what happens?

EVAN: And then some lucky guy gets to have sex with her in front of the rest of the crowd.

MICKEY: Nice.

EVAN: Not very. The second girl was given something, she was practically unconscious when he took her down.

MICKEY: Meaning no consent?

EVAN: Yep. The first one I didn't get a good look at, because I was still on early shift. I'm in an apartment upstairs of the club and there's a minicam rig, but it's stationary.

MICKEY: Gotcha. Why the big investment on this?

EVAN: Word is at least one of the girls never came upstairs again.

MICKEY: So you got live porn, rape, controlled substances, possibly kidnapping, possibly murder.

EVAN: And it looks so nice on the outside.

MICKEY: I'm surprised you're there by yourself.

EVAN: Actually, so am I.

Lights down. Drop downstage scrim. No projection. No music; just traffic noise.

A voice in the darkness:

CASSANDRA: Something bad happens, everybody says, just roll with it. All my life I've been rolling with it. But I've been in a box too long. I've got too many corners now.

Pull downstage scrim, then upstage to reveal

Scene 7. *Int.* The Blue Note, early evening. EVAN is at the bar. Dance hosts LARRY and SAMMY mingle with customers, as before. EVAN glances up at the "door" from time to time. Enter RUINED GIRL (FOX), on the platform. Cue music:

Song - One Time *(rumba; LARRY and SAMMY featured)*

RUINED GIRL

One time, all time
I remember
Loving you
you loved me
One night, all night
you were with me
Were we one?
You left me
How could we let all this
go when we had the whole
world in the palm of our hands?
I meant so much to you
you meant so much to me
how could we let this love end?
One time, all time
I remember
loving you
you loved me.

Exit RUINED GIRL to applause.

Scene 8. Enter CASSANDRA, stage right. She makes her way to the bar.

EVAN: Well, hello again. You just missed our star singer.

CASSANDRA: Oh really? What's her name?

EVAN: (thinks for a moment) Not sure. There's never an announcement for either singer.

CASSANDRA: You're a big help. Does she perform anywhere else?

EVAN: I think Ivory made a deal with her. She's exclusive to ... what?

CASSANDRA: (sotto voce) Shit. (normal tone) Did you say Ivory?

EVAN: Uh, yeah. Why? You know him?

CASSANDRA: I think I've heard of him. No big deal. (Fake smile.) Hey, is that Larry? I'd better get my dance while he's free.

> CASSANDRA catches up to Larry, they begin to dance to an instrumental reprise of "Dance with Me." Music is low for action following. EVAN watches between customers, not looking happy; SAMMY comes to the bar for a drink.

EVAN: Hey Sammy, nice dancing.

SAMMY: Thanks.

EVAN: Could you do me a favor later on?

SAMMY: Maybe.

EVAN: I want to dance, that gal dancing with Larry.

SAMMY: Oooh, barkeep's been bit.

EVAN: (laughs) Yeah, maybe.

SAMMY: Sure, I don't mind filling in for a few.

EVAN: I got some slippers back here so you can kick off the heels.

SAMMY: Wow, you think ahead.

EVAN: You're the only one here most of the time qualified to fill in. Man's got to take a break once in a while.

SAMMY: Just give me the nod.

EVAN: Sure will. Thanks a lot.

SAMMY: No problem.

> SAMMY tosses back her drink and goes to mingle as CASSANDRA finishes her dance and returns to the bar, slides onto a stool.

CASSANDRA: Crystal was right, he's a good dancer.

EVAN: Mr. T chains and all?

CASSANDRA: Hey, nobody's perfect. I'll put up with a lot for a decent dance.

EVAN: Which he can deliver. Cosmo tonight?

CASSANDRA: Um, actually it's been ... I'm pretty tired. Can I get a coffee?

EVAN: Sure. I'll make a pot.

CASSANDRA: Thanks.

EVAN: No problem.

Lights down briefly. Medley of background music to indicate passing time.

Lights up on CASSANDRA, draining her coffee cup. EVAN catches SAMMY's eye and nods.

CASSANDRA: I'd better go.

EVAN: Can I have a dance? If you're not too tired.

CASSANDRA: Oh, I think I can find the energy.

> SAMMY comes behind the bar and nudges EVAN out of the way.

SAMMY: Where's those slippers you promised me? … Oh, here. Aaaah.

EVAN: Thanks, babe.

SAMMY: Say no more. (To CASSANDRA:) Don't let him step on your toes.

CASSANDRA: I'll try to stay out of his way.

> Bar lights dim as EVAN and CASSANDRA dance to instrumental reprise of "One Time." Music ends and lights come up.

CASSANDRA: Thanks, that was nice.

EVAN: The pleasure was mine. Hey, um ...

CASSANDRA: What?

EVAN: I'd like to buy you dinner sometime

CASSANDRA: (brief pause) Do you have a night off?

EVAN: Sunday?

CASSANDRA: Where should I meet you?

EVAN: You know Maestro's?

CASSANDRA: Yeah, sure.

EVAN: Seven o'clock.

CASSANDRA: Okay.

Both smile. Exit CASSANDRA.

Scene 9. Bar lights dim, spot on EVAN. Cue music:

Song - Suspicion (Undercover Tango) (LARRY *and SAMMY featured)*

EVAN

My every move is self-defense,
my every word meant to deceive
I'm just collecting evidence
But I don't trust, I don't believe
and I suspect what I see
and I suspect what I hear
and I expect you to be
a danger if you get near
I watch your hands
I watch my back
I'm never sure
if you'll attack
it's all a risk
it's all a chance
it's all a part
of danger's dance
and I suspect what you do
and I suspect what you say
and I'm a danger to you
I don't expect you to stay
and when you go into the night
I'll never know if I was right

I watch you go *(instr)*
I watch you go

Lighting change, exit female Dancers.

Scene 10. *Int,* The Black Box. EVAN is behind the
bar but getting no business. Dance hosts are gone.
Howling pack of male customers pounds the tables.

HENCHMAN is in position by the stage. Black Box
Girls file on as we cue music:

Song - I'm the One *(cha-cha; much dirtier than their
previous number)*

BLACK BOX GIRLS

You look so lonely, mister - why are you sittin' here
alone?
You look so hungry, mister - you need a taste of
downtown
baby I'm the one
yeah! The one you want
yeah! The one you need
yeah! The one you - what you waitin' for?
You look so tired, mister - you need a place to rest
your head
you look so nervous, mister - you need someone to
calm you down
and I'm the one
yeah! The one you want
yeah! The one you need
yeah! The one you came here lookin' for
I'm the one to touch you, feel you, ease you
the one to hold you, scold you, tease you
the one who knows just how to please you

229

and you know it 'cause you know - baby I'm the one
you look so ready, mister - why don't we take a step
outside?
You look so steady, mister - but I can take you for a
wild wild ride
'cause I'm the one
yeah! The one you want
yeah! The one you need
yeah! The one you're followin' out the door now
baby I'm the one
yeah! The one you want
yeah! The one you need
baby I'm the one

*Lights down on scene. Drop double scrim.
Background music – Suspicion reprise. Upstage scrim
conceals Blue Note set. Downstage conceals set
placement for following scene. Draw downstage scrim
and bring up corner spots, fade music.*

*Projection – daytime street – on upstage scrim, fades
in and remains in place. Effects lights on phone
booths as they are in use, then off.*

Scene 11. *Ext* - street corners, stage left and right,
each with phone booth. Enter EVAN, stage left; dials
telephone.

EVAN: Hey Mickey, what's doing. Yeah, it's a safe
line. I've got some tape for you. Same drop? ... Okay.
Listen, I need to know if there's another department
working this case. Someone's been showing up for no
good reason. I think she's a civilian, but ... yeah.
Could be a relative, yeah. Cassandra Burke is the

name I got. Let me know when you're ready to move on this. See ya.

> EVAN hangs up phone and exits, stage left.

> Enter CASSANDRA, stage right; dials telephone.

CASSANDRA: Hey, it's Cassandra. Can you talk? This is the place all right. I think the bartender is a cop, undercover. I don't know if I should tell him the truth or ... well, I don't know what I'm going to do. I haven't seen her yet.

There are at least two singers, I haven't seen either one yet. I don't know if my girl sings, haven't had a chance to call her folks and find out. The other performers, they're all too old to be my girl. But I don't know who might have come and gone recently.

No, I'm not sure. Could you find out for me? I'm sure the name he gave me isn't ... Evan Michaels. And ... I'm having dinner with him in a few days. It would help to know before then. No, it's probably not a good idea. There's just something ... I like him.

Thanks a lot. 'Bye.

> CASSANDRA hangs up phone and exits, stage right.

Lights down on scene. Downstage scrim to hide set change. Music: I'm the One reprise. Projection: a different street scene. Music fades out as downstage scrim goes up. It is early evening, another day.

Scene 12. *Ext,* Maestro's Restaurant. A front of windows with an awning; cafe tables and a menu stand. EVAN is waiting. Enter CASSANDRA, stage right. He sees her at once.

EVAN: You made it.

CASSANDRA: Yeah.

EVAN: I'm glad.

CASSANDRA: (smiles) Me too. Can we sit anywhere?

EVAN: Sure. (They sit.) Listen, I have a confession to make.

CASSANDRA: Me first.

EVAN: You're not married, are you?

CASSANDRA: Funny, you're funny. ... I'm sure you've checked me out. Evan ... or whatever your name is ... look, I know you're a cop.

EVAN: Well, that's a relief.

CASSANDRA: So now you don't have to confess.

EVAN: And now you know I'm not working for that scumbag by choice. But there's something I need to know.

> Pause in conversation as a WAITER comes. Pantomime of ordering, etc. WAITER 2 brings drinks almost immediately after WAITER 1 goes inside. Exit WAITER 2, inside.

CASSANDRA: So?

EVAN: I need to know why you were looking for Ivory.

CASSANDRA: Don't you want to know how I know you're a cop?

EVAN: Your law firm. You've got a friend, I've got a friend.

CASSANDRA: Ah, dammit.

EVAN: (laughs) You did all right as a P.I. So anyway.

CASSANDRA: That star singer of yours.

EVAN: Yeah?

CASSANDRA: I think she's my daughter.

EVAN: Whoa.

> Pause for service. CASSANDRA and EVAN
> interact with WAITER 1.

EVAN: What happened?

CASSANDRA: Well ... this is the messy part. She doesn't know I'm looking for her. I'm not sure she knows I exist ... I gave her up. I was sixteen.

EVAN: Wow. I'm sorry.

CASSANDRA: It was just one of those things. And yes, I did all right as a P.I. I found her family. And I found out she left school, left college, right at the end of her first year. They had no idea what became of her. She just ... never went home. So I did some snooping around. Her friends at school ... they told me enough. She got into drugs. I think this Ivory person, his name kept coming up.

EVAN: I'll bet it did.

CASSANDRA: Please tell me he's going down.

EVAN: He's going down.

CASSANDRA: Thank you.

> Pause to contemplate the dinner neither really
> wants.

CASSANDRA: If I come back to the club, will it cause problems?

EVAN: Not for me.

CASSANDRA: I want ... I need to see this girl. She may not be Francesca.

EVAN: She usually sings only once, early in the evening.

CASSANDRA: Every night?

EVAN: Not every night.

CASSANDRA: Shit. Well, I can't hang around there all the time. I could stay close, though, if you could let me know.

EVAN: The land line isn't safe until we're about to finish things. But we're close, really close. You just come once in a while, early if you can. I'll find out what I can. If you miss her, when we're ready to go I'll call you the minute she steps on stage and we'll finish it then.

CASSANDRA: Okay. Evan ...

EVAN: Yeah?

CASSANDRA: Why would you risk maybe compromising your operation over this?

EVAN: Three reasons.

CASSANDRA: Give me one.

EVAN: If we get her out before the end, we have a witness. Want the others?

CASSANDRA: One more.

EVAN: I had to leave someone inside once, I don't want to do it again. Last one?

CASSANDRA: No. (Smiles.) Not yet,

Lights down. Drop downstage scrim over restaurant set.

Scene 13. Finale, Act I. *No set.* EVAN and CASSANDRA walk out in front of scrim at opposite sides of the stage. Use spots to highlight each actor as they are singing. Cue music:

Song - When I See You Again *(duet. Note: they do not sing *to* each other)*

CASSANDRA

I see you when I'm lying alone
and there's so many scenes playing out in my mind
I'm no longer sure that my heart's made of stone
and if I look too close, what will I find?
I see you now in all my dreams
you must be much more than you seem
or why should I see your face in the midnight neon haze
why should I see your soul in your silent, bitter gaze?
My dazzled eyes may be fooling me, but then
maybe I'll know when I see you again

EVAN

You could be all I'll ever need
and if you follow where I lead
could be you'll see through my mask,
through the things that I have done
and before I could ask, you could say that I'm the one
you really need. Maybe it's a dream, but then
maybe I'll know when I see you again.
Too many years I've been lying alone

Never daring to trust, dreaming dreams of the day
when suspicion and rage won't be all that I know
and I'll open my heart, for there must be a way

EVAN and CASSANDRA

Can I trust you with all I am
I'll give you everything I can
For I believe that with you
I could make it one more day
maybe next time I see you, I'll know just what to say
to make you see I'm on fire for you, but then
Maybe you'll know when you see me again.

Lights down.

END ACT I.

Act II

Curtain rises *on dark stage; side curtains and upstage scrim are pulled. A tiny amount of light on reflective curtain behind platform.*

A voice in the darkness:

IVORY: Broken hearts have sharp edges. Be careful; you could cut yourself.

Lights up to reveal

Scene 14 *Int,* The Blue Note. The RUINED GIRL stands on the platform. Customers and hosts ease into motion as we cue music:

Song - Without You *(rumba:* LARRY *and* SAMMY *featured)*

RUINED GIRL

I remember a secret smile that only we could see
and I remember a silent laugh we used to share
unaware of passing time that left us no longer together
I remember walking with you in the warm dark night
and I remember a time we spent so unafraid
the love we made was endless
and left me forever defenseless
without you
wandering lost in everywhere
counting my cost in tears
missing you, emptiness inside of me, loneliness for company
nothing's the same without you
I remember you held me close and said that you loved me
and I remember a quiet time that meant eternity

now it's gone, what's left for me?
'Cause I remember crying for you every night
it can't be right, I can't believe I said that I could live
without you
wandering lost in everywhere
wishing that you were here
and if you knew what I'm trying to hide
I know you'd be here again at my side
`Cause I remember.

RUINED GIRL exits to applause.

Scene 15. Enter CASSANDRA, stage right. She
crosses to the bar as the lights change, dancers engage
for instrumental reprise of "In the Night." Enter
SAMMY from upstage, goes behind bar.

CASSANDRA: Hi Sammy.

SAMMY: Hey. What can I get you?

CASSANDRA: What goes good with this song?

SAMMY: Huh, I don't know. Oh well, yeah. Here I
go.

SAMMY takes her time fixing the drink.

CASSANDRA: What is that?

SAMMY: Let's call it a Black and Blue.

CASSANDRA takes a cautious sip, screws up
her face.

CASSANDRA: Man! What did you put in this?

SAMMY: Dark rum, kirsch, and blue curacao. What's
it taste like?

CASSANDRA: Try it. (SAMMY sips)

SAMMY: Mmmm, cough syrup. (They laugh) So I'll bet you're looking for Evan.

CASSANDRA: Oh god. Do I look desperate?

SAMMY: Hell no. You did yourself a favor when you walked in here. He's definitely the pick of the litter. I'd be after him myself if I didn't have a good one at home.

CASSANDRA: You're married?

SAMMY: Better. Living in sin. (They laugh again.) Sorry though. He's off tonight.

CASSANDRA: Oh well. Guess I'll just take my medicine and watch the show.

SAMMY: Have fun.

      SAMMY moves off to serve another customer.

Scene 16. Regular SINGER takes the platform. CASSANDRA looks up intently, then LARRY crosses to invite CASSANDRA to dance. Cue music:

Song - If I Wanted Love *(waltz;* LARRY *and* CASSANDRA *featured)*

SINGER

You don't have to say you love me
I don't want to ask too much
You don't have to say that you'll stay with me
I just need to feel your touch
I know you don't need someone in your life
I have no romantic hopes
But when I get lonely these long long nights
I need you to hold me close
If I wanted love I'd try again

I don't dare believe it now
that this is the time that you are the one
I've got to stay free somehow
If I wanted love what would you say?
Could we ever work it out
Could this be the time
Could you be the one
Could this really be what love is about?
I can't think about the things we've done
I can't dwell on what we said
When we were together it felt so right
I'll try not to lose my head
I just can't make myself seek you out
I can't let this last too long
when I know one day you won't be around
one day it will all be wrong
If I wanted love I'd try again
I don't dare believe it now
that this is the time that you are the one
I've got to stay free somehow
If I wanted love what would you say
could we ever work it out
can this be the time
can you be the one
can I hope to say
I love you

SINGER exits to applause.
CASSANDRA watches her go, a slight droop in the
shoulders.

Scene 17. CASSANDRA returns to the bar, closely
followed by IVORY, who enters from upstage right,
followed by his HENCHMAN. She is a little startled
when IVORY speaks to her.

IVORY: I've seen you here before.

CASSANDRA: Have you?

IVORY: How d'you like my place?

> CASSANDRA's attention is caught now: she
> had not known him.

CASSANDRA: I like it. No TV.

IVORY: I prefer a live show myself. (looks her up and down) Have you seen Crystal's act?

CASSANDRA: Yes, the first time I came. She's great.

IVORY: She's one of my treasures. Good striptease is a dying art. So what brought you here that first time?

CASSANDRA: I moved to the neighborhood not long ago and I don't like drinking at home. So do you talk to all your newcomers?

IVORY: No. (beat) You're a little out of the ordinary.

CASSANDRA: (nervous) I guess so.

IVORY: Well, it's been nice meeting you. Enjoy the show.

CASSANDRA: Thanks.

> CASSANDRA watches the dancers
> (instrumental reprise, "The One You Want") as
> IVORY exits upstage left. SAMMY comes
> back to her.

SAMMY: What did he want?

CASSANDRA: I'm not sure. He was kind of creeping me out.

SAMMY: I'm not surprised. Ya know ...

SAMMY is briefly called away to serve
another customer. CASSANDRA waits
impatiently.

CASSANDRA: What?

SAMMY: Not that it's not nice to see you here, but
this isn't really a friendly little neighborhood bar.

CASSANDRA: What do you mean?

SAMMY: (checks her back) The show up here is
nothing like the show downstairs.

CASSANDRA: (low voice) What show?

SAMMY: Amsterdam.

CASSANDRA: You mean ... live?

SAMMY nods.

CASSANDRA: Oh my god. Oh don't tell me any
more. I don't want you to get in trouble.

SAMMY: Neither do I.

SAMMY moves away. CASSANDRA digs in
her bag for bills, leaves a few on the bar with
her unfinished drink, and exits right.

Lights down.

Scene 18. Int, The Black Box. Customers (male only)
are dim shapes on stage. The HENCHMAN is
downstage, looking straight out (menacingly) at the
audience. Bar lights go down and the Black Box Girls
file out, looking even nastier than last time, as we cue
music:

Song - One track mind *(tango)*

BLACK BOX GIRLS

Don't you look at the cracks on the ceiling
Don't you look at the trash on the floor
Don't you look very hard at your feelings
Never mind all the locks on the door
Keep a one-track mind, now you got what you wanted
Keep a one-track mind, close your eyes
Keep a one-track mind, you got what you were
looking for.
Took your time checking out all the merchandise
Took your time, chose the one who fit your plan
Now you got all night if you want to try it on for size
Take your time, you gotta be a man
Keep a one-track mind, now you got what you wanted
Keep a one-track mind, close your eyes
Keep a one-track, gotta get what you're paying for.
Don't even think about the woman waiting up for you
Don't even think about your children's eyes
You made your choice, now you're gonna get what's
coming to you
Gonna get down, claim your prize
Keep a one-track mind, now you got what you wanted
keep a one-track mind, keep it on your own business
one-track mind and don't think about tomorrow
one-track mind, close your eyes
Keep a one-track mind, now you got what you were
looking for.

Lights down on platform; bar lights remain.

Scene 19. *Int,* The Black Box, after closing. SAMMY
is cleaning up the bar. Enter IVORY from upstage
left.

IVORY: Good night, Sammy?

SAMMY: Not bad. I missed dancing, though.

IVORY: Thanks for pinch-hitting. Oh, and Sammy.

SAMMY: Yeah?

IVORY: Just tend bar, okay? No little heart to hearts with the customers.

SAMMY: Whatever you say, boss.

> SAMMY quickly finishes and exits left.

IVORY: And is she a mole, or is he a mole, or is the other one a mole; or am I just seeing things?

> Enter HENCHMAN, upstage right. Crosses halfway to bar.

HENCHMAN: Talking to yourself, boss?

IVORY: Sometimes I'm the only one who makes sense.

HENCHMAN: Anything booked for the Cave?

IVORY: That last one will be hard to top.

HENCHMAN: The next new thing will do.

IVORY: I suppose.

HENCHMAN: What are you gonna do about Fox?

IVORY: What do you mean?

HENCHMAN: She's getting weirder. Is she using?

IVORY: Not anything of mine, but how should I know?

HENCHMAN: Just thought you might. None of my business.

IVORY: That's right.

Exit HENCHMAN, upstage right. Foot light gels in hot colors light IVORY as we cue music:

Song - Speak no Evil *(boogie-woogie)*

IVORY

Yeah it's dark, and it's hot,
and the scum are coming out to play
find my mark, take my shot,
and it's always gonna go my way
when I see one on the lookout
that's when I throw my hook out
what's a suit doing down here
if he isn't looking to pay?
Yeah it's dark, and it's hot,
and my girls are climbing up the wall
and you're just what they want,
something handsome, something dark and tall
now with business getting brisk
hey, we're pros, this ain't a risk
over there, down the stairs,
stranger go and have yourself a ball
(raps)
You get what you pay for,
Do what you want to do
No receipts, no returns,
This isn't Saks Fifth Avenue
If you're worried what will people think
You haven't got a clue
Just handle it like business
'cause we're here to sell to you.
(singing)
Might not be what you like to admit

but I'm a business man
pass your laws, I won't quit,
there's no morals here in no man's land
I don't ask you to love me
just speak no evil of me
it's a service that you're paying for,
I only sell what you demand
I don't care if you love me
just speak no evil of me
You're as criminal as I am
even if you won't shake my hand
I don't want you to love me
just speak no evil of me
got your name and your number,
have a nice trip back to Wonderland.

Lights down. Double scrim drop for set change.
Projection: the café block. Music: One Track Mind
reprise. Downstage scrim comes up to reveal

Scene 20, *Ext,* Maestro's. CASSANDRA and EVAN
are seated, all the signs of a finished meal on the table.
They are sitting at right angles, not across from each
other.

CASSANDRA: I don't think I'd better go back there.

EVAN: I think you're right.

CASSANDRA: Did I blow your cover?

EVAN: I don't think so. I'm sure he's suspicious, but
let's face it; crooks are always suspicious. And he's
got a lot to lose.

CASSANDRA: Sammy told me about downstairs.

EVAN: Pretty nasty.

CASSANDRA: God, I hope your singer isn't Francesca. I'd rather not find her at all ....

EVAN: I got a picture.

CASSANDRA: What?! How?

EVAN: Hidden camera in the dressing room. Here.

> EVAN pulls a small photo from his jacket pocket, slides it across to her.

CASSANDRA: Oh ...

EVAN: Is it ...?

CASSANDRA: I ... can't be sure. All the makeup, and the hair. It could be. Her parents told me she could really sing, she wanted to be in a band but they told her no, not till she was twenty-one.

EVAN: Is there any other way I can ID her?

CASSANDRA: What, like a birthmark or something?

EVAN: Well, I'm not expecting to see her naked. A nickname, something like that?

CASSANDRA: Her roommate called her Fox.

EVAN: I'll ask around. (pause) I'm sorry.

CASSANDRA: Don't be sorry. You're going to help me get her out. Aren't you?

EVAN: She's under eighteen, right?

CASSANDRA: Just.

EVAN: Then we'd better move fast. But it's going to blow my op, so I've got to check in first.

CASSANDRA: Evan, you can't wreck your setup. Getting him is important.

EVAN: Look, there's one thing I've learned doing this shit and that is that there is always a new crook. It's like the science thing, nature abhors a vacuum, right? So does crime. As long as the demand is there, someone will find a way to supply it. But he will go down, one way or another, if we can get her out.

> CASSANDRA leans to close the distance and kisses EVAN.

CASSANDRA: You can't imagine what this means to me.

EVAN: She may not thank you for it.

CASSANDRA: I'm sure she won't.

> A silent pause, heavy eye contact.

EVAN: Want to go?

CASSANDRA: Yes, let's go.

Lights down. Pull both scrims for set change. Draw downstage scrim to reveal telephone booth, right. Projection – street. Sound effects.

Scene 21. Ext, street. Spot on booth. Enter EVAN stage right, goes to telephone and dials.

EVAN: My cover is getting thin. He's suspicious. Yeah, partly, but here's the thing. I've got a chance at getting one of the girls out. I'm not sure she'd testify, but even a deposition ... . I know that. I don't care.

Look, after what happened last time, I am not going to leave someone inside if there's any way around it. With everything I've given you, your case should be made by now. If it's not, it's not my goddamned fault. You keep dicking around and one day soon you'll pull me and the girl out of the river, and then where's your case? You better believe it. Yeah, trust me. I'll let you know when it goes down.

Lights down. Double scrim for set change. Projection – a skyline view. Music: If I See You Tonight reprise. Draw downstage scrim to reveal

Scene 22. *Int,* the office storeroom, minus police posters. CASSANDRA is leaning against a file cabinet, EVAN is seated at the table.

CASSANDRA: Mind if I ask how you found out?

EVAN: Invasion of privacy. (pause) Actually, your contact and mine turn out to be the same guy.

CASSANDRA: (surprised laugh) Well, that makes coordinating things easier.

      CASSANDRA paces restlessly.

EVAN: It'll be over soon.

CASSANDRA: How do you stand it!?

EVAN: I'm used to it. And I'm not involved usually … not like this.

CASSANDRA: What's the worst way something like this ever went wrong?

EVAN: Oh, Cass, you don't want to hear that.

      CASSANDRA looks at him.

CASSANDRA: No, I guess not.

EVAN: Come here. (stands up)

      CASSANDRA goes to him fast, he holds her tightly; not a kiss, just comfort.

Lights down. Double scrim for set change. Projection – city traffic at night. Music: Speak No Evil reprise. Draw both scrims to reveal

Scene 23. *Int,* The Blue Note. EVAN is behind the bar. Dancers are tangoing to instrumental reprise of "One Track Mind." Enter SAMMY upstage left, whispers to EVAN, who picks up the bar phone.

EVAN: Cass. She's on in five minutes. Get here if you can.

> EVAN hangs up phone. Polishes glasses, polishes the bar, serves a few customers. Enter CASSANDRA in a hurry, right, just as music ends.

Spotlight on platform as RUINED GIRL (FOX) steps through curtains at back of platform. CRYSTAL enters stage left and brushes off a customer who approaches. CASSANDRA watches, frozen, as we cue music:

Song – The Way to Die *(waltz – no dancers)*

FOX

The veil is taken from my eyes
I wander past the nights I've never seen
The lights are dim, the streets are still
I wonder why he had to kill my soul
He took me in and made me whole
then broke me down and made me old
He taught me life in all its pain
Then gave me ignorance again
He made me whole and numbed my mind
then broke my heart and blinded me to love
The king is dead, long live the king

from underground the third rail sings to me
A razor blade that knows my name
a pistol shot in a soldier's game
the rage and shame I wear inside
the sweet release that cannot hide from me
Too soon, before the sun awakes
I'll find the place, I'll find the way to die.

> Dancers applaud and EVAN moves quickly to
> the platform, jumping up to take FOX by the
> arm. CRYSTAL moves to FOX's other side,
> reassuring. CASSANDRA moves up as FOX
> resists EVAN.

CASSANDRA: Fox?

FOX: What? Leave me alone!

CASSANDRA: I need to talk to you just for a minute.
Can we step outside?

FOX: What for?

CASSANDRA: Just for a minute. Please.

FOX: Who are you?

> CASSANDRA backs up a little, holding out
> her hand. FOX allows EVAN and CRYSTAL
> to guide her to the door. Exit FOX, CRYSTAL
> and CASSANDRA.

Scene 24. Enter IVORY, upstage right, his
HENCHMAN close behind. EVAN turns to face him.

IVORY: Where is my little star going?

EVAN: She's getting to know her mother.

251

IVORY: Her mother? You mean the teenage slut who threw her away wants to get all cozy now she's middle aged and guilty?

EVAN: You can put it that way if you want.

IVORY: I'll put it any way I please.

> Regular SINGER comes on to platform; seeing trouble brewing, she steps off, signaling, and does a fade. Instrumental reprise of "When I'm Not With You" comes up. Customers, oblivious, begin to dance around IVORY and EVAN.

IVORY: You can't take her away, you know.

EVAN: She's a minor. Didn't she tell you?

> IVORY's face tells the story: he's in deeper than he thought. HENCHMAN does a fade.

IVORY: Who the hell are you to mess with me. You are fired.

EVAN: Thanks. Here's your keys. (Tosses them; IVORY catches them by reflex) If I'm not mistaken some colleagues of mine are out in the alley. If we go out and talk to them I won't have to make a scene, disrupt your customers' evening.

IVORY: "Some colleagues."

> EVAN fishes a badge out from under his shirt.

IVORY: You and your cop friends can go to hell. You got nothing.

EVAN: You wish.

> Exit IVORY and EVAN upstage left, passing SAMMY. She flashes a thumbs-up at EVAN, turns it into the bird for IVORY.

252

Scene 25. Music ends and lights change to Black Box dress. Female customers exit. Black Box girls come on, looking worn-out and ill-used, as we cue music:

Song - Alley Cat *(cha cha)*

BLACK BOX GIRLS

Alley cat on a hot tin roof (watch your step)
Alley cat on a lonely street (watch your back)
Alley cat just scratchin' to stay alive
Kicked out the door one too many times
Now you don't even try to get in
Folks pass you by and they close their minds
don't want to see past your skin
You're a sad sight for sore eyes; what can one person do?
Left behind by every ride
now you don't even try to get on
folks pass you by and they push you aside
if they can't see you you're gone
You're a kick in the conscience; what can one person do?
They can't even meet your eyes
Alley cat on a hot tin roof (watch your step)
Alley cat on a lonely street (watch your back)
Alley cat just struggling to survive
These are the streets where the careless die
and no one steps aside to help
Everything's for sale and everybody lies
Every man's out for himself
We're a threat to the system; what can one person do?
There but for the grace of God - go you.

Lights down. Double scrims for set change. Projection – café block. Music – One Time reprise. Draw downstage scrim to reveal

253

Scene 26. *Ext,* Maestro's. CASSANDRA and FOX are seated across from each other at a table. FOX is leaning away from her mother, arms and legs crossed. CASSANDRA leans forward, but appears relaxed.

CASSANDRA: I know this is the worst possible way to have introduced myself. Your parents asked me to help find you.

FOX: I was doing fine.

CASSANDRA: That would be why your songs are so upbeat and happy.

FOX: (defiantly) Ivory was going to make me a star.

CASSANDRA: I'm sure he told you that. What did he tell the other girls?

     FOX glares silently.

CASSANDRA: Do you want to get some dinner?

FOX: No.

CASSANDRA: How about some dessert? Coffee?

FOX: What are you trying to do, make me like you?

CASSANDRA: I don't care if you like me, but it'll give you something to do with your hands.

FOX: (astounded) What do you mean you don't care?

CASSANDRA: Okay, that was a lie. I do care. But I don't expect you to. There's a lot of shit going under our respective bridges right now, and this isn't the time to start scooping it up.

FOX: My mom - .

Awkward pause.

CASSANDRA: It's okay, she is your mom.

FOX: She'd fall over dead before she'd say "shit" in front of me.

CASSANDRA: It's a personality thing. (signals for a waiter.)

> WAITER enters, leans to CASSANDRA for instructions, nods, exits again. FOX and CASSANDRA wait in silence till WAITER enters again with two coffees and a slab of cheesecake. Exit WAITER.

CASSANDRA: Look, help me eat this, okay? Stress makes me hungry and then I get fat.

FOX: Me too. (looks surprised at herself, then frowns)

CASSANDRA: Eat first, then yell.

FOX: What ... .

> FOX snatches up a fork and digs in, scowling. CASSANDRA takes a few half-hearted bites, then watches, hiding a smile behind her coffee cup.

CASSANDRA: Still want to scream at me?

FOX: I probably will later.

CASSANDRA: That's okay.

Lights down. Pull both scrims and bring up blue-tinted lights on empty apron. Projection – street. Sound effects.

Scene 27. *No set.* Enter EVAN, left; and CASSANDRA, right.

CASSANDRA: What happened?

EVAN: It's done, textbook.

CASSANDRA: Oh, thank god.

EVAN: Turns out we got Sammy and Crystal both to roll over on him. Sammy's going to be managing the place for a while.

CASSANDRA: Thank you. Thank you so much.

> EVAN and CASSANDRA meet in the middle and embrace.

EVAN: How's she doing?

CASSANDRA: Angry. Sad, confused, anxious, but mostly angry.

EVAN: At you?

CASSANDRA: Oh sure. But I think there's something to work with. Her parents picked her up at the station.

EVAN: And how are they?

CASSANDRA: Over the moon. They're taking her straight to rehab. And how are you?

EVAN: Glad to be standing right here.

CASSANDRA: Me too.

Scene 28. Act II Finale. Cue music:

Song - Never alone *(rumba)*

EVAN

Alone, again; facing another night in an empty bed again;
listening to the questions inside my head:
should I call? Do you want me as I want you?
If I fall, will I ever be free of you?

CASSANDRA

Alone, again; watching the neon lights flash across the
wall again; counting the minutes hoping that you
might call - or should I?
Could my loneliest night be done?
If I fall, after all, there's a chance you could be the one

EVAN and CASSANDRA

Why should I be alone tonight?
When I know where you are
Why shouldn't I just go to your side
Where I know you won't turn me away
And I'll find the right words to say

EVAN and CASSANDRA

Why should we be alone tonight?
Here I am; here you are
we've come so far into the light
and we've left all the darkness behind
now we've given our word
and we've given our hearts
and we've given our hands
Never alone again.

Finis

*****

About the Author

Alexandra Caluen lives in a small purple house with her husband, a bottle of Laphroaig, a lot of books, and nine pairs of ballroom shoes. She works in patent law and has enough hair for three people.

www.thelastories.com